Beshert

*Nancy —
Thanks for
reading!
♡♡♡
Erin*

ERIN GORDON

>>>>>>>>>>>>>>>>>>

ALSO BY ERIN GORDON

Cheer: A Novel

Heads or Tails

AUTHOR'S NOTE

BESHERT IS A MODERN ROMANCE, SET IN THE Middle East, featuring themes of identity and faith. Two of those elements – the Middle East and faith – are complex. Underrepresented in American novels, Israel is a tiny country with spectacular food, people, history, museums, topography, and innovation. At one time or another, each of Israel's neighbors has sought to obliterate it. Conflict also exists within Israel's borders, particularly between the ultra religious and the secular and between the government (a democracy) and its Arab citizens. Beshert's main characters – one American, one Israeli – were born into different faiths and are grappling with how much, if at all, faith should influence their lives. While Israel is the backdrop for this story and the characters' religious differences create tension, Beshert is, above all, a romance novel. As such, this story is not meant to reach definitive conclusions about international relations in the Middle East. This...is a love story.

"Again she had the feeling that things were beginning to lose their focus in her soul."

– Leo Tolstoy, *Anna Karenina*

Chapter One

*F*or the first time ever, when the jet hit the runway, Chelsea didn't even flinch. Her sister, on the other hand, clutched Chelsea's arm as if it were her only hope of remaining in the living world.

"I hate this part!" Baylee announced, unnecessarily, through gritted teeth.

"It's fine," Chelsea said wearily, keeping her eyes on her book. She simply didn't have the energy to worry that they'd slam into the side of a building or another plane, just like she didn't have the energy several hours ago to worry, like Baylee did, that a terrorist had snuck onto the flight or that the pilots were drunk. Plus, she was two-thirds through *Eat Pray Love* and wanted to keep reading right up until the fasten seat belt sign dinged off.

The plane's back tires met the asphalt and the jet hurtled forward, resulting in the unsettling shriek of an object lurching past the laws of physics and out of control. Chelsea noted it, thinking that if her life were making a sound, that's precisely what it would be.

"Let's pray," Baylee commanded, squeezing her eyes shut and sliding her hand from Chelsea's forearm to clasp her fingers. "Dear Lord," she

1

began, sounding, Chelsea thought, so much like their father. "We thank you for bringing us safely to this moment, for letting us have these last hours together before our separate journeys begin. Please continue to bless us with your grace as we travel onward. And please spare us from flight delays, lost luggage and turbulence. In Jesus's name, Amen."

"Amen," Chelsea whispered. Never once in her life had she not concurred with "Amen" at the end of a prayer. Though she was smack in the middle of the biggest crisis of her life – faith and otherwise – she wasn't about to start going rogue on Amen now. She was in doubt, to be sure, but she was no cynic.

The jet finally began to slow and Chelsea tore her eyes from her book. She thumbed its pages while gazing out the window. Newark was hazy in the August late afternoon, glowing and dirty. Sunlight barely slid through the low clouds and she couldn't tell whether it was hot or cold outside. The landscape was industrial and gray, a marked contrast from Colorado, her lifetime home of twenty-seven years that she'd left a few hours ago. She removed her hand from the book and began to twirl the gold stud that had newly adorned her upper ear cartilage, a piercing that none of her family or friends approved of. It was still healing and the first crusty turn made her eyes water. She raised her eyebrows and looked up, not wanting a tear to disturb her eyeliner. Her makeup had to last at least another fifteen hours, her expected travel time to Tel Aviv. She made a mental note to touch everything up in the ladies room after she parted ways with Baylee.

The plane slowed further and Chelsea heard her sister exhale and then watched her excitedly pack up her carry-on bag with the God's Hands Christian Ministry logo printed on the side. In Touch magazines, a stack of psalms and devotionals cards, a packet of "Skinny You" tea.

As they pulled up to the gate, Chelsea turned on her phone and noted that everything had adjusted from Mountain to Eastern Time. She wondered what time it was in Israel. She wondered what she'd be doing if she were still in Colorado Springs, if she hadn't just flipped her life upside down by launching this pilgrimage. She wondered what, if anything, would still be there for her when she returned weeks from now. Where would she live? How would she pay rent? Would her dad speak to her? Stasis wasn't an option, she knew. But she also had no idea how she'd move forward once she returned. For now, moving forward meant only getting away. Clarity was what she hoped to find in the Holy Land.

Texts began rolling in.

Honey, remember, be safe. I love you. You are God's precious creation. From her mother.

Take pics! I hear the beaches R amazing! Can you bring me a postcard from the Church of the Holy Sepulchre? And some bagels? (Bagels are Jewish, right?) From her best friend Crystal.

How can you leave? Me? Us? You can still turn around and come back. From Austin.

Chelsea shuddered, shut the screen off and began packing up her own things. *Eat Pray Love.* The navy leather notebook where for years she'd been writing down her favorite bible passages – she hadn't made an entry in weeks. Cinnamon hard candy. Her laptop with the peeling Ashes United and Manifest stickers, remnants from her short-lived rebellious phase when she listened to Christian punk bands.

The terminal was crowded – it was late summer, after all – and smelled of cooking grease. Baylee was three steps ahead of her gazing around as if the Newark airport were an interactive museum display. She seemed so small in her knee-length denim skirt and red flats, her baby fine blond hair captured in a neat pony tail.

"Hey," Chelsea said, quickening her pace to catch up and tug on her sister's bag. Baylee turned and they both stopped, the crowd whooshing to and fro beside them, different languages peppering the stale airport air. "Are you going to be okay? Are you nervous? Excited?"

While Chelsea would soon be boarding a plane to the Middle East, Baylee was heading into Manhattan to meet up with young missionaries from all over the United States and Canada. The following day, their group would travel to Guatemala where they'd spend eight weeks helping medical professionals at a Christian hospital and gaining hands-on experience in "evangelism and discipleship." Their family had done mission trips before – to El Salvador and Haiti – but Baylee had never gone alone. Although Baylee was twenty-two and had just graduated from Colorado Christian College (the alma mater of pretty much everyone in their family), Chelsea still thought of her as her baby sister.

"Of course I'm excited," Baylee said. "Jesus has led me to this moment and I trust Him."

Chelsea sighed inwardly and twisted her new earring. Had Jesus led Chelsea to this same moment? This same, terrifying, unsettled moment? Or had Chelsea defied divine intervention and messed up her life all by herself? She didn't know who she could trust anymore. Certainly not herself. She no longer knew about Jesus.

She squeezed her sister's hand. "You're right. You'll do great."

"You could come with us," Baylee said. "Pastor Stanton says, 'You find yourself when you forget about yourself.' You'll find peace in our community."

Chelsea moved her head, half-way between a nod and a shake. For a moment, Baylee looked hopeful, like she was about to achieve victory – to be the person who'd finally convinced her sister to abandon this unnecessary journey. No one believed that a solo trip to the Middle East was what Chelsea needed to right her upside-down life. But Chelsea knew she needed clarity. And the only way to get that was by putting distance between herself and the life she'd been groomed to lead, the only life she'd ever imagined for herself.

"No." Chelsea set her jaw, looked her sister in the eye and forced out the response she knew she must. "For once, I have to do not what is easy, but what is hard."

Baylee's face fell. "My word, Chels! Your life *has* been hard for months, ever since–"

"–I appreciate your efforts, Baylee," she interrupted. Chelsea was on a precarious cusp, one that she didn't want to be drawn back from. She spoke as much to herself as to her sister, using a football analogy the way their dad would. "I'm first and goal from about four yards out...."

Baylee maintained her pleading expression.

Chelsea took a breath and reframed her statement in a way that would force Baylee to reduce her resistance. "Philippians three, thirteen: 'I'm off and running, and I'm not turning back.'"

》》》》》》》》》》》》》》》》》》》

TWO HOURS LATER, AFTER HUGGING BAYLEE GOODBYE, retrieving her luggage and going through the most extensive security screenings she'd ever experienced, Chelsea was at the gate waiting to board her flight to Tel Aviv. She held her book in her lap but couldn't tear her eyes from the hodgepodge throng of fellow waiting passengers. There were tall men in black pants, long black coats, tall black hats and long black beards. Like her, they held books in their hands, but they also swayed forward and back as they read, periodically whispering and glancing down at the pages. There were families who looked like they were from California, fully clad in t-shirts and flip flops. There were women about her age – beautiful women with full lips and flawless skin – with their hair wrapped in something...turbans? There were little boys with long, tight curls, but only on the sides of their faces. There were men that Austin would have derided as "tech bros" talking on cell phones and typing rapidly on tablets. Chelsea's heart thumped and her throat grew dry.

What was she doing with these people?

She hadn't even left the United States but already she felt very, very far from The Springs where nobody looked like this, where everyone was just like her.

With fifteen minutes until boarding, Chelsea gripped the handle of her carry-on and made a final bathroom run. What had been defiance when she was with Baylee had morphed into real fear and her legs trembled as she waited in line for a stall. When she washed her hands, she leaned into the fluorescent-lit mirror to get a closer look at the stud in her upper ear, its glistening appearance still surprising her. So far, no signs of infection. She pulled back a little, swept her light brown hair to one side and wondered whether she could really pull this piercing off. Exhaling, she modified that doubt. Really, could she pull any of this off?

For the first time in her life, Chelsea wasn't convinced God could work it out. But deep down, she still hoped he would.

Chapter Two

*N*oam stood panting on the sidewalk as the bus approached. By his calculation, if he'd indulged his co-worker in the conversation about Bnei Yehuda's latest soccer win instead of holding up a palm, announcing "Shabbat Shalom" and cocking his thumb behind him to indicate he had to leave, there's no way he'd have made it to the bus stop on time. He'd sprinted the two blocks from his office as it was. And this was not a bus he wanted to miss. It was Friday afternoon and Israel – even secular, cosmopolitan Tel Aviv – was about to shut down until sundown Saturday. This approaching electric bus was the last pre-Shabbat bus traveling north along Efal Street. Noam was too tired to walk the two miles to his Migdal Street condo in Neve Tzedek. And on principle he only forked out the shekels for a mo-neet in three situations: he'd had too much to drink, he was carrying heavy art supplies too unwieldy to take on the bus, or it was fewer than three weeks since a suicide bomber attack on the same line.

Looking like something a Jedi might travel on, the sleek blue bus came to a quiet stop and Noam waited to board behind other tech workers, Haredim, thirty-something moms corralling kids, and grandmothers carrying aromatic roast chickens in canvas bags. Shabbat was imminent.

He swiped his transit pass under the sensor and headed to the back of the bus. It was just seven stops to his house, but with pre-Shabbat traffic and all these passengers, it could take as long as twenty-five minutes. Noam was eager to park himself down and not move. As usual, he was weary from lack of sleep and nearly desperate to get home so he could sketch, the only thing that helped him unwind. It was undeniable that he needed some kind of help, but he had no idea what kind of physician or therapist could help him, given that he'd never heard another soul complain of the same...affliction. He hadn't been this bone tired since his years as a basic training squad commander, when it was his job to transform a bunch of wild eighteen-year-olds into soldiers prepared to protect this tiny, ancient country from the dozens of military powerhouses that wanted nothing less than to obliterate the world's only Jewish state. Looking back, Noam sometimes wondered how he made it through those years. On the spectrum of Hawk to Dove, he was most decidedly a Dove. And when it came to Judaism, he was without question the least observant Jew on the base. But Noam did believe in Israel and his years training new soldiers, while conscripted, had been among his happiest.

Making his way to the second-to-last row on the bus, he passed groups of Haredim and Yeshiva boys. He took a seat beside a woman whose thick, dark curls were piled on top of her head, with uneven tendrils escaping to frame her phone's ear buds. Noam hoped that she wouldn't need to get off the bus before him. He was, as his mother would say, falling-off-his-feet tired, one of the many expressions that harkened back to her Texas childhood.

Settling into the seat, he closed his eyes and thought about what he'd sketch that evening. Lately, he'd been focused on baseballs and donuts. He was obviously in a circles phase. But someone had brought a slab of chocolate halva to the company conference room earlier that day and Noam had thought the chiseled rectangular shape and crumbly texture would provide a welcome challenge, one tiring enough that he might actually catch a few pockets of sleep before sunrise.

Just as the bus pulled away from the curb, Noam sensed the curly-haired woman's movements next to him. He opened his eyes and she nodded, indicating that the next stop was hers. He forced his lips into a half-smile and stood to let her pass to the aisle. He slid over to the window seat and gazed outside. It was late August in Tel Aviv and heat waves wiggled vertically amongst trees and between buildings. Like most Israelis, Noam was inured to the heat, regarding it almost like a comforting old friend that accompanied him everywhere. The smell of perspiration – his and others' – went entirely unnoticed. But non-natives, like his American-born mother, never got used to the Middle Eastern climate. "It's hotter than a Laredo parking lot," she often said while blotting her hairline with a damp paper towel.

At the next stop, the curly-haired woman stepped down the back-door stairs, new passengers boarded and the bus started up again. Noam shut his eyes, longing to rest even for a few moments. But then, out of nowhere, the low din of Hebrew, Arabic and English conversations was suddenly punctuated by yelps and huffs. Noam turned away from the window, observing some sort of scuffle a few rows ahead. His long-ingrained commander training kicked in and he sat up alert to get a better look. A Hasidic man stood in the aisle with a furious, almost hostile expression. He spoke loudly, his salt-and-pepper beard shaking with each word. "Ayk ath m'ez." *How dare you.* His companions, seated nearby, along with nearby Yeshiva boys, shouted in angry agreement, "Ya! Ya!" Even two Israeli Arabs seemed astonished.

The object of their derision was a woman with thin, straight hair a color that could only be described as honey. Though her back was to him, Noam could tell from her backpack and the style of her shorts that she was American. Suddenly, he realized what was happening. He leapt to his feet, determined to rescue her.

"Zeh beseder, zeh beseder," he said, dashing up the aisle towards her. *It's alright, it's alright.* "Hya amryqayt, tyyrt!" *She's American, a tourist.*

The woman turned toward him, her face stricken.

"It's okay," he said, nodding assuredly. "They can't.... Here, come with me." He wrapped his hand around her upper arm, which was so delicate his fingertips practically touched his thumb. He pulled her towards him, feeling her shaking, and guided her back to his row.

"It's okay," he said again once they sat down. "They're Hasidic."

She looked at him blankly. He'd never seen eyes like hers before – they were large and perfectly, exquisitely almond-shaped. She framed them with too much eyeliner and mascara, but they were undoubtedly beautiful. Noam made a mental note to buy almonds to sketch.

He inhaled. "They're Orthodox Jews. That means they're very religious. *Very* religious. It's why they dress like that and look like that."

"Why did they yell at me?" the woman asked, her voice faintly cracking.

"Did you try to sit next to one of them?"

She nodded and he noticed that her eyes were not just the shape of almonds, but the color too. They blended stunningly with her honey-colored hair. She looked like some kind of sweet Israeli dessert that hadn't yet been invented in the land's five-thousand years.

"According to their practices," he explained, "men and women cannot touch each other unless they're married. No shaking hands, nothing. By trying to sit next to him, you threatened to violate that."

"Oh my goodness!" she said, looking abashed. "Should I go apologize?"

Noam smiled. Who *was* this woman?

"That's not necessary. I guarantee you, they haven't had this much excitement in weeks. It'll give them something to gossip about at Shabbat dinner tonight. Plus, you don't speak Hebrew."

"No," she smiled back at him, looking more relaxed than she had a moment ago. "But you do."

"Like I said, not necessary. Look," he said, jutting his chin towards the front of the bus, "they're getting off anyway. See? They've already forgotten about it."

Relief flooded her face and she leaned back in her seat.

"First time in Israel?"

She nodded. "How'd you know?"

"Wild guess."

She smiled and Noam noticed that everything about her face was perfectly proportioned – her wide-set eyes, her full, bow-shaped lips – except one of her front teeth, which was slightly cockeyed and chipped.

"So these...what did you call them?"

"Hasidics."

"Hasidics. They're Jewish?"

He nodded.

"How are they different from other Jews?"

"What do you mean?"

"Well," she said, "is anyone else on this bus Jewish?"

He rolled his eyes dramatically. "Everyone on this bus is Jewish." He paused and exaggeratedly took in the other passengers. "Except those two men three rows up."

She sat up to get a better look at them. "Are they Christian?"

"Israeli Arabs. Muslims."

"How do you know?"

"I just do," he said almost crossly. "What's your question, exactly?"

"So essentially everyone on this bus is Jewish. And I can sit next to other people, other men, but not the...Hasidics?"

"You're sitting next to me."

"You're Jewish? Your English is perfect."

"News flash: Jews speak English."

"I mean, I didn't even think you were from here. So I didn't assume you were Jewish."

"My mom grew up in Texas and always spoke English to us. I had two first languages: Hebrew and English." This get-to-know-you conversation, this banter felt pleasantly familiar to Noam – like taking a bite of a long-ago favorite childhood snack. Chatting with this woman reminded him how long it had been since he'd met someone new. Of course, he'd dated since Adi, but no one, even the women he'd been set up with on blind dates, had felt as entirely new to him as this woman did. She'd upended his plans to simply zone out as he traveled toward home, but as he chatted with her, he also felt calm and secluded from the frantic pre-Shabbat bustle.

"So how can you and the man who yelled at me both be Jewish?"

"What's your name?" he asked.

"Chelsea."

"Of course it is."

"What's that supposed to mean?"

"It's just.... I've spent a lot of time in the States. I might have guessed your name was Chelsea or Ashley or Brittany. Are you from the South?" He observed the small gold cross around her neck, which glinted in the late afternoon light, as did the small stud in her upper ear, which seemed to Noam rather out of place given the rest of her dress and demeanor.

"Colorado."

He nodded knowingly.

"What's *your* name?" she asked, betraying slight annoyance.

"Noam. Spelled N-O-A-M but pronounced as two syllables."

"It's nice. What does it mean?"

"In English, it means 'pleasantness.'"

She smiled. "You're pleasant, if a little brusque."

"In other words, I'm Israeli."

"Back to my question: how can you and the man who yelled at me both be Jewish?"

Noam exhaled slowly. This woman had no idea she was asking precisely the question he'd been struggling with for the last several years.

"Chelsea," he confessed, "I have no idea."

Chapter Three

Chelsea woke Saturday morning after a hard, dreamless sleep. She'd been in Tel Aviv for thirty-six hours and had met up with her tour group, Christian Holy Land Journeys, the evening before. Others in the group, mostly Americans like herself, had complained of crushing jet lag, but Chelsea couldn't relate. She'd slept on the plane, she'd slept the first night in the hotel and she'd slept again last night. It was as if her body had been aching to align itself in this ancient Middle East time zone. Either that or living with shame and terror was grueling and no match for jet lag.

Her fellow tour mates felt as familiar to Chelsea as the new time zone did. Among them was a middle-aged Kentucky couple who shared the same unflattering haircut, a family from Beijing, two thirty-something single men from Chicago who seemed to be on a hunt for wives. Christian Holy Land Journeys had pitched itself as unique among tours visiting Israel, an extended, multi-week trip filled with "fellowship, faith and fun." But it was the faith element that had appealed most to Chelsea. The last several months had tested her faith like never before. Even her teenaged rebellion against the religion her parents had taught her paled compared to what she'd experienced lately with Austin, her father, with her whole world view. How could she be a Christian if that's what *they* were? If Jesus forgave their sins, why couldn't she, too, forgive what they had done? And what kind of God excuses such gratuitous cruelty?

When she'd decided to leave, to rip the picture of her future in half, somehow she knew the Holy Land was where she had to go. Others might try to sort out their lives in places like Italy or Bali – that's what the woman in *Eat Pray Love* had done after all. But Chelsea knew that ideology was at the root of her crisis. She needed to view Jesus's life path for herself to see if she had been, still was and could continue to be a Christian. She knew in her bones that, at twenty-seven, she needed saving all over again – or to completely abandon the only life she'd ever known.

Her mother had objected, of course. She'd excused Austin and her husband, quoting to Chelsea Colossians Three Thirteen: "Bear with each other and forgive one another if any of you has a grievance against some-one. Forgive as the Lord forgave you." She wanted Chelsea to simply tape up the tear in the family picture they'd snapped so many years ago. Plus, her mother feared that traveling to "that Jewish place" would mean Chelsea would somehow return with a tail or horns. She hadn't explicitly said that, but Chelsea sensed it nonetheless.

A text alert chimed on her phone. She rolled over and grabbed it from the nightstand.

Arrived safely in Guatemala. Praise God. Staying with a lovely family. Miss you. B safe!

Chelsea tapped out a breezy, reassuring reply to her sister. She didn't mention yesterday afternoon's embarrassing faux pas on the bus. She'd had a few hours to kill before the tour group met for the first time in the hotel conference room that evening and figured she'd hop on a metro bus to experience a little flavor of Tel Aviv, a city that served primarily as the tour's meet-up and departure location since most of the country's Christian sites were elsewhere. Not only had she inadvertently violated a principle tenet deeply held by several odd-looking Jewish men, but she'd also met an interesting local man about her age. His name was Noam and although his English was excellent, he seemed nearly as foreign to Chelsea as the Hasidim (as she'd learned they were called). He was black-haired, with eyes the color of the Mediterranean, and at least seven inches taller than she was, maybe more. He had hairy, muscular forearms and a sculpted, athletic build. But she didn't text Baylee any of this.

She checked the tour schedule and threw on boyfriend jeans – Oh, the irony, she thought – and a sweatshirt for breakfast. At the elevator bank, a sandwich board sign had been placed next to the far left elevator. It read, "Shabbat Elevator."

"What the heck does that mean?" a man's voice boomed from behind. She turned and saw the same-haircut Kentucky couple. He was pointing at the sandwich board.

"Oh, I read about this!" the wife announced proudly. "You know how in Europe everything shuts down on Sundays? No grocery stores open, blah, blah? Well, here, their 'day of rest' is Saturday. And some people take this so literally that they don't do any work – not just *work* work but any work like turning on a light, using a pencil or even pushing an elevator button! So these elevators are pre-programmed for those people. They stop at every floor. Ta da! No buttons need to be pressed."

At that, the designated Shabbat elevator opened as if on cue. It was empty. Chelsea and the couple exchanged a glance, then shrugged and got in.

"What about walking?" the man asked, as the elevator traveled to the floor below and opened. No one got in. It continued. "Does walking count as work? What if a pregnant woman goes into labor on the day of rest? Isn't that work?" He winked at Chelsea. She smiled back at him, but the lighthearted exchange made her feel alone.

The wife giggled. "We'll have to ask our tour guide about these ins and outs!"

Chelsea assumed the Hasidic men from the bus followed those strict Shabbat rules. To her surprise, she also wondered if Noam did too.

Downstairs, the hotel lobby was bland and generic, likely a precise replica of the chain's Philadelphia, Cleveland and San Francisco locations. This disappointed Chelsea, who wanted every moment of this journey to feel different from the life she'd known before. But the Hyatt was what Christian Holy Land Journeys offered. At the start of the buffet line, a sign read, "Dairy Shabbat Meal." Chelsea wasn't sure what that meant exactly but she did notice that all the food was cold and there were no meats of any kind. She loaded up her plate with familiar items – yogurt, cottage cheese, a muffin – and some foods that didn't seem breakfast-y at all – olives, hummus and something called halva. She took her plate outside to the patio and deliberately selected a small table with a single seat. She was still getting acclimated to this path she'd chosen and there'd be plenty of time for socializing in the coming weeks.

Before diving into her food, she took in the scene. The Hyatt was about three blocks from the shore, but the patio had an unobstructed view of it. It was only nine-fifteen in the morning but the beaches were already filling up. Perhaps this, she thought, is what Israelis did on their day of rest – relaxed on the beach. The sea, not quite green, not quite blue, was calm that morning. Seagulls squawked overhead, a sound that Chelsea had disliked since she was a child visiting relatives in Galveston. The ocean had always made her feel unmoored, like she was on the edge of some-thing. Land-locked Colorado had always felt safer, the expansive moun-tains serving as a protective hug of sorts. Closer to where she sat, four stray cats roamed the patio and then together hopped the small gate to the street beyond.

Chelsea picked up her fork and then hesitated.

"Thank you, Father. Amen," she quickly whispered. Her faith was shaky and she was here in Israel to test it, but some habits were hard to break. It made her wonder how much of her faith was based on belief and how much was simply that: habit.

An olive for breakfast seemed weird, but Chelsea adopted a When-in-Rome attitude. She stabbed it with her fork and bit into its thick, smooth meat, experiencing an explosion of briny juice. She was used to sliced black olives from a can that she sprinkled over enchiladas. She'd never tasted one so flavorful. She forked another and swirled it in the hummus. More saltiness, this time creamy. She closed her eyes and inhaled.

"Coffee?" a waiter asked, startling her out of her food bliss.

"Uh, yes, please."

He poured a small cup of what looked like engine grease. She twirled the new ear piercing and leaned down to sniff. It smelled spicy, like her grandmother's cardamom walnut squares. She took a sip. It was so smooth and rich that tears sprung to her eyes. She followed the olives and hummus with a few bites of cottage cheese. Then she tasted the halva, which instantly broke into sugary, nutty shards in her mouth.

Two twenty-something men, who to Chelsea looked Italian or maybe Greek, walked onto the patio holding hands. They selected a small table nearby and scooted the chairs so they could sit next to rather than across from each other. They continued holding hands as they ate and Chelsea wondered if the one on the left really was left-handed or just ate with his fork in that hand to accommodate the affection. She shifted in her seat and looked away, back towards the Mediterranean.

The couple brought to mind Beth, Chelsea's former co-worker in the marketing department of Colorado Springs General Hospital. They started there the same week, the first real job for both of them. Beth was two years older (having taken a gap year before college and then working as a part-time ski instructor in the months after her December graduation) and a whiz at what was then a new tool for marketing: social media. Beth was tall and "big-boned," as Chelsea's mother might say. Her blond haircut was not unlike Austin's – cropped close to her face, which was very, very pretty, complete with flawless olive skin, symmetrical dimples and, as Chelsea would come to tease, freakishly white teeth. In the first days at the hospital, they attended the mandatory three-day training, which included instruction on privacy laws and the proprietary computer system. The training was taught by a nerdy, humorless and expressionless middle-aged man who had a propensity to say "Tuesdee" and "Wednesdee" instead of Tuesday and Wednesday. They gave each other the side-eye, stifling giggles, and a bond was set. For the next two years, Chelsea and Beth enjoyed weekly "Tuesdee" lunches together and laughed often about other absurdities of their jobs. (They once drafted, for their eyes only, a press release and Facebook post boasting about the hospital doctor who'd operated on the wrong knee. The patient had written "Not This One" in pen on his shin but the "Not" had been washed off during pre-op. Whenever Chelsea or Beth was sad or upset about something, the other inevitably pulled out the fake press release to cheer her up.)

Once, Chelsea asked Beth why she kept her blond hair so short. "You should grow it out – it's so thick and lustrous. It'd frame your face nicely," Chelsea said.

Beth explained that she was proud to be "butch," a term she introduced to Chelsea. That, Chelsea realized then, explained Beth's shapeless Levi's and the navy button-downs with not even a necklace to adorn her outfit.

She was Chelsea's first lesbian friend ("That you know of," Beth liked to quip) and it took some time for Chelsea to process. She was relieved that Beth had a long-scheduled vacation the week after the revelation. Chelsea had always been taught that gay people were sinners who needed salvation. The Bible, the word of God, was explicit on that point. But she also cared deeply for Beth, who vocally supported Chelsea's ideas in team meetings, who kept her company during the long and sometimes boring work days. She knew that Beth volunteered every weekend at an animal shelter and once a month at a shelter for battered women. Beth was even using part of her meager hospital salary to help pay her younger sister's college tuition. It was confusing that someone like that, someone with so much goodness, was also so unquestionably a sinner in the eyes of Christ.

When Beth returned from vacation, she suggested they have their "Tuesdee" lunch on "Mondee" instead so they could catch up.

"Howya doing, kid?" Beth asked as she unwound a burrito from its foil. "I know this butch thing came as a surprise and is contrary to your beliefs." That was another thing Chelsea admired about Beth – she was direct, she didn't mess around.

"To be honest, I'm a little sad. It must be difficult for you to live like that, not only as gay but without Jesus."

"I'm pretty happy."

"I know." It was true. Beth was one of the most even-tempered, good-natured people she'd ever known.

"Do you feel differently about me now?"

"No, no," Chelsea said emphatically, placing a hand on Beth's forearm. "I don't agree with the gay lifestyle. But because of Jesus, I'm compelled to love all people. God has made all people, including people like you."

"Do you pity me – because *I* don't have Jesus?"

Chelsea hesitated. "Not exactly. Christ is my saving grace from all my sins. What he gives me is a profound comfort. It makes me want to share that. Because I care about you, I want you to have that too. And I'm sad that you won't."

A few months later, Beth was let go. It turned out that hospitals didn't really need a social media presence – people came to hospitals because that's where their doctor practiced or where an ambulance took them; they simply didn't choose hospitals based on Instagram posts. After Beth left, the hospital kept its social media accounts and it was Chelsea who was in charge of updating them once in awhile with innocuous photos of the refurbished cafeteria or a cardiac nurse celebrating a twenty-year anniversary with the hospital.

Back on the patio in Tel Aviv, Chelsea heard a disapproving *tsk* from behind. She glanced over her shoulder and saw the couple from the elevator abruptly shoving their chairs back to leave the patio with their still full plates.

"Men who practice homosexuality will not inherit God's kingdom," the woman said in an ostensible whisper that was clearly intended to be heard.

Chelsea bowed her head and squeezed her eyes shut. She'd heard Austin declare those same words just a few weeks ago at a press conference. She gulped down more coffee and wondered whether she could sort things out here after all.

Chapter Four

One of the many reasons Noam lived in Tel Aviv, instead of his hometown of Haifa an hour north or in the Ramat Aviv suburb where his orthodox sister lived with her brood of seven kids, was that Tel Aviv was a secular city. True, much of the city, including shops, museums and public transportation, shut down on Shabbat. But he could still get his favorite chicken shwarma and sachlav, a hot milk-based drink topped with pistachios, raisins and coconut, at Nehama Vahetzi, a cafe open every day except Yom Kippur, the holiest day of the year. Even the many atheists Noam knew – and he was beginning to count himself among them – observed Yom Kippur either by fasting, attending shul services or both. Yom Kippur was still several weeks away and Noam hadn't yet decided how he'd observe, if at all, this year. At the very least, he'd do some atoning. He planned to apologize to his mom for occasionally being short with her on the phone ("Oh, puh-lease," she'd probably say, grabbing his head between her hands and kissing his forehead profusely. "You're the best boy in the world for even calling me in the first place."), to his sister for being a day late in wishing his nephew Kiva a happy third birthday, and to his colleague Ben at Statyst for snatching his favorite mug from the office kitchen and sending email ransom notes, hoping to score one of Ben's court side seats to Bnei Yehuda in exchange for return of the mug. Everyone in the company thought the ransom messages were hilarious but Ben simply purchased a duplicate mug online and never invited Noam to a game.

Hebrew pop boomed from speakers in the ceiling corners of Nehama Vahetzi. To Noam, that music was tinny and erratic, too electric and club-y for his taste. But because he spent nearly every Saturday afternoon at Nehama, he knew that Daniel, his favorite barista, would soon be arriving for his shift. Daniel had the best taste in music. He'd introduced Noam to black gospel choirs from the American South, which blew Noam's mind. It was rhythmic and communal (he loved the claps and feet stomping), blues-y, sad and euphoric. Noam began sketching and painting along to it, and his work instantly gained an intensity and dimension it hadn't had before.

In addition to being open on Saturdays and having the best sachlav in the neighborhood, Nehama was Noam's favorite cafe because they showcased his paintings. It was a two-story industrial-type space with large white walls perfect for displaying enormous canvases and pleasingly grouped collections of smaller pieces. One of Noam's friends knew the owner of Nehama and knew he was eager to add unusual but accessible art to the otherwise cold, bland walls. Noam's friend thought Noam's realistic, colorful paintings of sports equipment, donuts, candy wrappers and dilapidated American and European storefronts would be perfect. Nehama's owner agreed. Art was merely a hobby for Noam – working as a statistician at Statyst was his profession – but he sold a few paintings a month from the exposure he got at the cafe. And that enabled him to purchase high-end art supplies and huge canvases guilt-free.

Noam approached the counter right as Daniel was taking over. That meant Noam would get an extra frothy sachlav and soon his favorite gospel would be piped through the sound system. He took a seat in the upstairs loft area. In addition to sketching to Daniel's playlist, Noam enjoyed observing the cafe scene. Saturday afternoon at Nehama Vahetzi was decidedly secular, filled with beach-goers coming inside for the day, tourists enjoying downtime between afternoon tours and dinner, hipster couples wearing babies in slings. Noam also enjoyed the occasional window into how his work was perceived. Once, a tech millionaire-turned-Israeli cabinet minister went bananas over Noam's five-foot square painting of a cut pomegranate that was hanging on the stairway wall. He inquired about its availability and Daniel pointed out that the artist happened to be sitting in the cafe at that very moment. Not only did the man pay Noam in cash for the painting right then and there, but he took it off the wall himself and carried it right out the door to his black Suburban.

Noam took a sip of his sachlav, tasting the hint of orange blossom that was Nehama's signature ingredient, and pulled a sketchbook from his satchel. Still lifes were his specialty, which was one reason he forced himself to sketch scenes at the cafe. He wasn't great at drawing people. Even when they posed, they were always in motion – a large inhale, a relaxing of the jaw were subtle changes that could alter what he'd started. It frustrated Noam. He liked precision – in his art, in everything. It's why he became a scientist. It's why he never like the Humanities in school. Too many *interpretations*. Noam operated in absolutes.

But he was aware of these tendencies of his and was committed to stretching them. So the sketchbook was where he let himself experiment with things like figure drawings and landscapes. He drew in black pen, then went home and added watercolor. That, too, was part of the experiment. In paintings, Noam favored primary and secondary colors, which to him were the world's original, truest colors. But with watercolors in his sketchbook, he forced himself to blend. What in an acrylic painting would be green became brown mixed with hints of yellow – an olive hue – in his sketchbook. It felt unnatural, but he made himself do it anyway.

Today, he zeroed in on a lower corner of Nehama by the window. He began with big shapes – the rectangle of the window peppered with ovals of the nearby tables. Then he focused in on the hard part – the people. At one table sat a typical Tel Aviv hipster – bald head, laptop, ear buds. At another table, two middle-aged women were gossiping. He could tell by the way they leaned in close to each other, periodically looking around furtively and then giggling. Noam carved shallow slanted lines in his sketchbook. In the furthest corner, Noam spotted a woman sitting alone reading a book. Her spine was curved, almost hunched, as if she wanted to dive into the pages. A backpack rested at her feet. After a moment, she lifted her head to sip her drink. Noam couldn't see her face but somehow she felt familiar. He observed a moment longer and realized why. Her hair – it was the color of honey or the freshest, sweetest Israeli date. He'd seen that lustrous, shiny hair before. It was the woman from the bus.

Noam put down his pen and watched her. For several minutes, she continued to simply read and sip her drink. Periodically, she'd pause and gaze out the window, watching the foot traffic on Amzaleg Street outside. Once, he thought he saw her wipe her eyes. But maybe she'd just been scratching an itch. He couldn't tell. Something about the woman was mesmerizing to him, but he had no idea why. She looked nothing like women he had dated in the past, certainly nothing like Adi, whose athletic body and thick blond hair he'd loved. He tried to resume drawing, even picking another spot in the cafe and starting over. But it was no use. He just wanted to watch Chelsea. That was her name, he remembered. *Chelsea.* Honey-haired, chipped-toothed, Christian, American Chelsea.

A few minutes later, she got up and grabbed her backpack. Noam momentarily panicked at the thought of her leaving. Should he run after her? For what purpose? He shook his head to clear his insane instincts. Why in the world should he go after her? And say what, exactly? he asked himself. Aydyvt. *Idiot.*

But Chelsea wasn't leaving. She stood, scanning the cafe, clearly looking for the restroom. As she glanced around, Noam was tempted to bow his head. But he didn't. Instead, he looked right at her, hoping that

26

would somehow inspire her to gaze up and recognize him. But that didn't happen. After a few seconds, she walked towards the restroom underneath the loft area where Noam sat. While she was gone, he leaned forward over the railing to spy what book she'd been reading. *Eat Pray Love.* What was that? he wondered. Probably some sort of Christian fiction, he guessed.

A few minutes later, she returned from the restroom. But instead of going right back to her table, she paused. Noam wondered what she was doing and then realized she'd stopped directly in front of a collection of his small paintings. They were some of his favorites: still lifes of crumpled binder paper, an arrangement of three sliced mangoes, a balled-up sheet on an unmade bed, a half-empty box of paper clips, and a bowl of Honey Nut Cheerios. She moved in close to each one, so close she could pucker her lips and kiss the canvas. He wondered whether she liked them.

Suddenly, to his surprise, Noam started packing up his things. What was he doing? He'd barely begun drinking his sachlav. But it was as if he were propelled by outside, unseen forces. He tucked the sketchbook under his arm, grabbed his mug and walked down the stairs, forcing himself not to take two at a time.

As he approached her, Noam felt his pulse in his jaw. He sidled up next to her. The cross around her neck glistened under the cafe lights. His own body sizzled.

"What do you think?" he asked.

"They're extraordinary," she said, keeping her eyes on the canvases. Then she turned to look at him. Her eyes grew three sizes when they met his.

"Oh, wow," she said. "It's you."

"It's me." He smiled widely at her and silently cursed himself for what had to be an entirely goofy expression. But he couldn't help it. "How's your trip here so far? Upset any Hasidim lately?"

She let out a small laugh. "Ha. Not since yesterday. But I'm still a little on edge, not knowing all the customs." She turned back to the paintings. "I love these. The primary colors – they're so vivid. They're still lifes but somehow they have energy and movement. They're simple but also so realistic and precise. I can't imagine how hard it would be to paint something like this."

"Mmm...," he said in mild agreement. She couldn't know that her comments absolutely thrilled him, filling his body with a palpable warmth from head to toe. Was it merely her reaction to his work or the woman herself?

"Noam, right? Pronounced in two syllables?" she asked, looking up at him with her large, curved eyes. Like yesterday, she wore far more eye makeup than was necessary.

"Yes. And you're Chelsea. From Colorado."

She nodded. "Thanks for remembering. I'm sure you told all your friends about the stupid American girl on the bus."

"Not all my friends, but most. I'm still making my way through my contact list."

"Very funny."

"I thought so. So," he added, holding up his cup, "may I finish my drink with you?"

"I, uh, I'm just reading over there...but sure." He thought that perhaps he was intruding but she started moving towards her table by the window.

"Wait," he said, placing a hand on her shoulder. She spun around, looking at him as if she'd been burned by his touch. "Which of these paintings is your favorite?"

She crossed her arms and studied the five canvases anew. He didn't care what her answer was. He appreciated the opportunity merely to observe her. He was intrigued by this stranger. He didn't want to be, but it was reflexive.

"Mmm...probably the one with the bed sheet."

He nodded. "Here," he said, handing her his cup, "hold this." He placed his fingers on the edge of the painting and gently lifted it from the wall.

"What...what are you *doing*?"

"Don't worry," he winked. It was an involuntary gesture, something he wouldn't have done if he'd had the ability to control himself. "I can paint another one just like it."

Chapter Five

*n*oam reached toward her, and Chelsea had twin urges to swat him away and to clasp his hand, to feel the warmth of his long fingers. Before she could decide, he lifted the book that lay before her. She was both relieved and disappointed that it was the book he'd been reaching for.

"What are you reading?" he asked.

She quickly moved her hand, suspended in mid-air, to her head, smoothing a non-existent stray hair. "*Eat Pray Love.*"

"What's it about?" His Israeli accent was slight – far less than the waiters, cab drivers and shopkeepers she'd encountered so far in Israel – but it was apparent nonetheless. Certain words were jagged and harsh, full of Z's and guttural CH's that one simply didn't hear in English.

She widened her eyes. "*Eat Pray Love* – you don't know it? It was a big bestseller ten or fifteen years ago. Julia Roberts was in the movie."

"Best seller in your country. I haven't seen the movie. Is it a Christian novel?"

"What?" she said. "No, no. It's a true story, a memoir by a woman who goes on a trip of self-discovery after a divorce. Italy – that's the 'eat' part. The 'pray' part is actually about her time in India – she does yoga and stuff. She falls in 'love' at the end – in Bali. My grandmother...she, um, recommended it to me."

"You like?"

There, he sounded foreign. She looked down at her lap and swept imaginary crumbs off her pants. "Yes, I do like it. I always like my grandmother's recommendations." Then she added, "So you're an artist?"

"I make art. I sketch and paint," he said, shrugging.

"So...yes?"

"Actually, no. I'm a scientist. Art is just a hobby."

"Your paintings are amazing – so detailed, almost like photos. So don't say 'just.'" She observed a reddening of his cheeks. She was about to ask what kind of scientist he was, but he spoke first.

"So you've survived your first Shabbat in Israel? No more clashes with Hasidic men?"

She laughed even though the memory of yesterday's blunder still made her cringe. "There's still time, right? How many more hours before it's over?"

He looked not at a watch or a clock, as she expected, but out the window and up towards the sky. "Probably about four."

"What happens on Sundays?"

"What do you mean?"

"Are things shut down then too?"

He exhaled with a small chuckle. "Chelsea, you're in a Jewish state. Sunday is really, really a regular day."

With anyone else, she might have felt chided. But while Noam was succinct and direct, his words and manner carried a benevolence she couldn't deny. She especially loved the way he emphasized his points with repeat phrases like "really, really."

"Right," she nodded, pursing her lips and looking out the window herself. There was something...electric...about this man, who was so unlike anyone she'd encountered before. He was tall, dark and handsome in a way that was completely unlike the American stereotype of the same description. He was more than six feet tall, at least three inches taller than Austin. His curly hair, which wasn't exactly long but hovered around his ears, far longer than Austin's spikey blond crew cut, was not just dark but black. His blue eyes and his face exuded kindness, and the five o'clock shadow, which had probably sprung about two o'clock, lent a virile maturity to his whole appearance.

"What's your tour got planned for tomorrow?" he asked.

"Good question." She pulled the multi-page itinerary from her bag. "Sunday... Sunday... Oh, of course. We've got a church service in the morning. And then the House of Simon the Tanner in Jaffa in the afternoon."

"You can go to church anywhere. You're in Israel, the most remarkable little country in the world. Let me take you around tomorrow morning. I can show you things you will not see on your tour – on any tour."

Her heart thudded and she felt her cheeks growing crimson. She'd come on this trip to test – no, to rediscover – her faith. It was beyond what she'd experienced in high school when run-of-the-mill teen angst forced her to examine whether she followed Christ because she was truly saved or simply because her parents were Christians. Now, she came to the Holy Land to study Jesus's life first-hand. Going to church here was part of that – it was on the tour's agenda for a reason. She leaned back and glanced down at the book her grandmother had sent her. Eat. Pray. Love. A rebellion of sorts bubbled inside her, not unlike that brief period during freshman year of high school when she'd refused to attend church youth

33

group events and got her ears pierced at the mall, even though her mom had always quoted Corinthians Six Nineteen and declared, "Do you not know that bodies are temples of the Holy Spirit, who is in you, whom you have received from God? You are not your own."

She considered Noam's offer as she spinned the new stud in her upper ear. Leaving an organized tour – a tour with a thoughtfully plotted schedule, a tour using a professional bus company, a tour with *insurance* – was risky. Yet here was an unexpected opportunity to see a new country from a local's perspective. And, she thought, when was the time to do something totally out of one's character, if not on vacation on the other side of the world? Plus, Noam was right: if her journey went as she planned, she'd spend the next two thousand Sundays or more in church.

But where would he take her? A synagogue?

"Um...." Chelsea stalled, still resisting her strange urge to be with this man. But his attentive eyes bored into her. She leaned forward and he did too, reaching for her paperback. He held it up and toggled it back and forth, making it dance, making her laugh. Could she be so easily swayed away from Jesus? Perhaps *this* was among her tests on this journey.

"Okay," she exhaled. "What time should I be ready?"

>>>>>>>>>>>>>>>>>>>>>>>>

ONE SATURDAY DURING CHELSEA'S JUNIOR YEAR OF HIGH school, she spent the day at Pulpit Springs Church with Baylee, her best friend Crystal and four dozen other kids from nearby towns as part of a winter church retreat. She'd attended her first retreat the year before and loved it – the get-to-know-you games (state your name with an adjective of the same letter – Joyful Jenna, Graceful GiGi; unsurprisingly, "Murderous Maggie" did not return the next year) and the social time spent with faith-minded peers. She and Crystal made good friends at that first retreat and even visited them over the summer.

At the second retreat, Chelsea sat with her navy notebook on her lap, pen poised in her hand, though she hadn't written anything. Nothing had yet interested her. The pastor speaking was from a church in Pueblo. He was young – maybe early thirties – and Chelsea had been eager to hear from him. But she was quickly disappointed because his youth did not influence his speaking skills – in fact, he proved ten times more boring than the first speaker, who'd been her grandfather's age. Within two minutes, Chelsea began to zone out, her mind bopping from stress about her upcoming Chemistry quiz to frustrated indecision about whether to wear red Converse or silver sandals to that night's dance, at which Six Days, one of her all-time favorite Christian rock bands, would perform. She stole a look at the clock on the wall to the left. Seven more hours until the dance. Restless and sleepy at the same time, she crossed and recrossed her legs.

Suddenly, she felt a gust of wind pass over her. She lifted her chin to the ceiling, wondering why the air conditioning would turn on in the middle of winter. But that wasn't it. She turned to Crystal, flashing her a "did you feel that?" face. But her best friend remained motionless and continued to stare impassively at the pastor. Then a jolt of heat traveled up her spine, settling at the base of her neck. In an instant, the sounds of the room grew faint, yet her hearing sharpened. A voice spoke.

"You think you know me. But do you really know me?"

It was then that Chelsea understood that whatever was happening was happening solely to her. She didn't move. She held her breath and didn't even blink.

"Let's not just go through the motions," the voice said with precision and clarity. *"Let's have a real relationship."*

Lightheaded, she stood and discreetly shuffled past the aisles of chairs on her way to the bathroom, hoping that no one would observe her trembling. Once in a stall, she went over the words again. *You think you know me. But do you really know me? Let's not just go through the motions. Let's have a real relationship.* Her body shook and quiet tears dropped down her face.

She knew that Jesus had spoken to her.

After the Pueblo pastor's speech concluded, Chelsea opted for silent study instead of the bible trivia competition. Crystal was annoyed because they'd been quizzing each other for weeks in preparation. But Chelsea begged off, needing to process what Jesus had done. She'd gone from terrified to curious. She headed straight for the church library, joining two other kids who'd also opted out of trivia.

In her notebook, she wrote down the words she'd heard so clearly, circling them and then drawing lines out from that circle, filling the lines with her interpretations. For a half hour she wrote this way, then she opened the book to a new page.

"I've been going through the motions of church, the bible and prayer," she wrote. "I have a religion, things I do. But I've been a robot and it hasn't meant much. I want a real relationship with Christ."

She paused and looked up. One of the other kids was asleep with his head on top of his backpack.

"I want to be more than just a good Christian," she wrote and then concluded in capital letters, "I HUNGER TO TRULY KNOW GOD."

That night, she attended the dance as planned. Crystal had come in second in the trivia contest and, together they danced gleefully to Six Days hits like "Divine," "Abide" and "True." Chelsea understood that a permanent shift had occurred that day, a day that she'd will herself to conjure in her darkest moments in the years to come.

The next several weeks were spent in a bubble of faith, the winter break from school allowing Chelsea to read non-stop. Baylee begged her to join her sledding or skiing but Chelsea declined, instead spending hours devouring her bible and reading every post by her favorite Christian bloggers. Craving depth and substance, she pored over pages from her navy notebook. Often, she was confused. "I've never read this passage before," she'd think, even though every word was in her own handwriting. She filled new notebooks writing about Jesus and how his life would guide her own. She felt almost unbearably happy.

No longer an infant believer, she moved through life with a new, acute awareness that Christ was with her always – *always*. She maintained a constant dialogue with him in her head and in her heart. From that day on, Jesus became not just a vague notion imposed on her by her parents or her pastor. He became her cornerstone.

>>>>>>>>>>>>>>>>>>>>>>>>>>

CHELSEA GOT DOWN TO THE LOBBY OF THE TEL AVIV HYATT A few minutes before nine the next morning. ("On time is actually ten minutes late," her grandmother – a stickler for manners – always instructed.) Fellow travelers whooshed through the revolving doors, hitting her with blasts of Middle Eastern air, thick as hummus, every few moments. Noam had suggested they meet closer to ten, but she wanted to be out of the hotel before the rest of her tour group began gathering in the lobby for the bus to church. Plus, she suspected that if she got herself ready and downstairs, she'd be less likely to chicken out. She continued to sleep well in Tel Aviv, but her last thought before dozing off and the first thought when she woke was whether she had done anything crazier in her life than getting into a car with a stranger in a foreign country.

At the front desk, she scratched out a quick message on a piece of Hyatt notepaper and left it for the tour guide. She considered writing "not feeling well" or "too jet lagged" or "eager to be alone this morning," but none of those were true, and not lying was another principle her grandmother had imparted. She settled on, "Won't be joining the group this morning. See you later." She'd almost written "see you for this afternoon's lecture," but didn't want to make a promise, didn't want anyone to count on her. Chelsea wasn't sure if that had something to do with the rebellion she'd been feeling lately about all kinds of external expectations...or with wanting to leave her options open with Noam.

A small but sleek navy car pulled up outside and Chelsea saw Noam wave to her from the driver's seat. She pushed through the revolving door, surprised at the lightness she felt in her body and, more surprisingly, her mind. The gravity of what had happened at home, the panic of not knowing what kind of life she'd return to wafted up and out of her skull, like smoke through a chimney. She paused outside the door and inhaled the salty seaside air. Perhaps the lightness she was feeling had to do with spending the last few days at sea level. She was used to Colorado's oxygen-thin mountain air.

"Boker tov!" Noam said in greeting. He was wearing grey cargo shorts and a plain navy t-shirt that matched the color of his car. His hair was weighed down with the dampness of a recent shower, the black ringlets hanging lower than usual. He smelled...she couldn't place the scent. Was it sandalwood? Rosewood? They were smells she knew from an essential oils kit she'd purchased from a college friend who was a consultant with a multi-level marketing company. Chelsea hadn't been particularly interested in oils but she'd wanted to support her friend. The day she packed up her belongings from the apartment she'd shared with Austin, she filled a diffuser with peppermint and lemon oils, attempting to purify the apartment of her history there and maybe even wipe clean her own mind. Maybe it was spicy notes of frankincense that Noam smelled of. Whatever it was, Chelsea was struck by an aroma of manliness.

"Say it with me: bo-ker tov," he continued. She repeated after him. "Good. That means 'good morning.'"

She rolled her eyes to accompany her grin. "Yes, I figured." She buckled her seatbelt and nodded that she was ready. "How'd you sleep?" It was a question she and Austin unfailingly asked each other every morning.

Noam gripped the steering wheel and pressed his lips together in what looked like annoyance, and Chelsea feared she'd asked too intimate a question. He turned his head to the left, ostensibly to check for traffic, even though they were at a red light heading straight ahead out of the hotel driveway. Maybe she should have gone to church with the tour group. Getting in a car with a Jewish Israeli man had not been on her itinerary when she'd planned this mission to rekindle her relationship with Jesus.

"Where are we going?" she course-corrected.

The light turned green and Noam accelerated, his face softening to its normal relaxed expression.

"I will start by taking you to one of my favorite Tel Aviv sight-sees. You will see," he said. She inwardly giggled at his misuse of *sight-seeing* and her belly flipped involuntarily at the notion that there'd be more than one stop in their time together. As odd as it was to feel connected to a stranger, something about Noam filled her with curiosity.

They were mostly quiet as he drove through Tel Aviv. Noam hadn't been kidding – Sunday was a regular day in Israel. The traffic was heavy and horns blared. She felt as out of place in this big cosmopolitan city as she did the first time she'd first experienced the streets of Manhattan as a tween on vacation with her family. In sharp contrast, The Springs was quiet on Sunday mornings, with cars obediently traveling to, inevitably, one of the town's hundreds of churches. The contrast made her question again what, exactly, she was doing. She realized that was a question she actually should have asked herself long before – about Austin.

"Here we are," Noam announced as he turned into a parking spot.

She looked around. "We're where?"

Noam pointed to a nondescript small white building that might have passed for a medical office in Colorado Springs. "Independence Hall. It's where the state of Israel was founded."

They jaywalked across the street, Noam's hand resting protectively on Chelsea's upper back. When they reached the sidewalk and he removed it, her scapula still felt hot from where he'd touched her. They waited in line behind two families – one British, one American, both with small kids wearing circular head coverings. Noam paid the shekels for the entrance fee, joking in Hebrew with the woman behind the desk who giggled and looked away shyly.

They walked into a small, windowless screening room where they watched a film in English about the afternoon of May fourteenth, nineteen-forty-eight, just hours before the British Mandate of Palestine was scheduled to end, when Jewish leaders proclaimed the establishment of the state of Israel. The film flashed photos of older men, some with long beards, who read the Declaration of Independence, recited a Hebrew blessing and sang Hatikvah, a Hebrew song that became the new country's national anthem.

"I feel so stupid," Chelsea confessed when the film ended and they moved toward another room, Declaration Hall, where these historic events had taken place. "I thought Israel had always been Israel. Like in the Bible." *And he arose, and took the young child and his mother, and came into the land of Israel. Matthew Two, Twenty-two.* "But this country is not much older than my dad." She dipped her chin at the thought of her father, wondering whether he'd even speak to her when she returned.

Noam nodded. His hand was on her back again and Chelsea involuntarily slowed her steps ever so slightly to prolong his touch.

They sat down onto a rickety wood bench and listened to recordings of the United Nations' plan to partition what had been known as Palestine.

"They pulled chairs from nearby cafes," Noam whispered, leaning close but training his eyes on the two blue and white Israeli flags that hung vertically to frame a huge black-and-white photo of one of the bearded old men, Theodore Herzl. Noam told her about the Haganah, the first real army of Israel, and how it somehow won the Arab-Israeli war that began just one day after Israel's declaration of independence. Noam spoke quietly but with notable reverence.

"I am really, really a Dove," he explained with a passionate but quiet intensity that stirred her as much, if not more, than the fire and brimstone preachers she'd grown up with. "But I love this period in history. The bravery of the resistance fighters, Herzl's idealistic vision, the seeds of today's society that were planted then by gutsy decisions of a few men and women with a noble vision."

"Amazing, the risks they took," Chelsea agreed, noting how she herself always chose the safe route – where to go to college, what kind of job to have. Breaking up with Austin and traveling across the world to Israel was truly the first time in twenty-seven years that she'd chosen not to keep her world small and predictable.

"Zionists, they knew what they wanted Israel to be," he said. "Its magnitude was not unlike your country's revolutionary war with England."

That he brought up the founding of her own country struck Chelsea as a bit eerie. Just weeks ago, as her life with Austin was unraveling, she coped with restlessness by flipping channels on TV, one night landing on a documentary about the American revolution. The interviewed historians had wildly conflicting opinions about the impact of some battle or another, of Washington's judgment, of what the revolution's precise turning point was. One expert had said, "When studying history, the question isn't 'What?' but '*So* what?'"

Though Chelsea was an adult who'd graduated from high school with good grades and had earned a marketing degree from Colorado Christian College, it had simply never before occurred to her that history could be *interpreted*. She'd always just accepted that things had happened the way she'd heard – that Jesus had risen three days after his death, that Columbus had discovered America. It struck her that night that maybe events and truths she'd long accepted were not, in fact, absolute. She wondered, not without a glint of terror, what else her sheltered, manicured life had shielded her from. Days later, she made the irreversible decision to halt the trajectory of her own life.

41

Sitting on that old wooden bench, Chelsea turned to Noam, looking directly into his eyes for the first time that day. "What," she asked, "is a Dove?"

He stood and jutted his chin, signaling that she should rise too, that they were onto something new. "Chelsea," he said with a smile so wide and beautiful it almost scared her, "we obviously have a lot to talk about."

"But Marjorie had little use for any version of the faith. She regarded it as a body of superstitious foolishness perpetuated, and to some degree invented, by her mother for her harassment."

– Herman Wouk, *Marjorie Morningstar*

Chapter Six

*n*oam had once heard his American cousins use the phrase "game changer." Usually he believed that Hebrew or Yiddish phrases – klutz, mensch, schlep, shmatte – were far superior than English at precise descriptions but game changer perfectly captured what the day with Chelsea was to Noam. He'd been to all those places before – Independence Hall, the Palmach Museum, the Florentin neighborhood – with school, with the army, with visiting relatives. But he'd never been there with an American girl, a shiksa no less. Those locations always filled him with pride about Israel and Tel Aviv but today it was more than that. It was pride mixed with an unfamiliar stirring that he hadn't felt in a long time. Maybe ever. The charged feeling came partly from being an Israeli who loved his country. But part of it came from Chelsea herself – those lovely-shaped eyes, that one tooth, her quintessentially American turns of phrase like "Oh my word" and "It's hot enough here to peel house paint."

"You're incredible," Chelsea said back at his apartment in Neve Tzedek at the end of their day together. Noam felt himself glowing red, then realized she was referring to his paintings. He'd suggested they eat dinner at Dallal, his favorite Arab restaurant two blocks from his house. He'd been going there for years and the owners showcased one of his paintings behind the hostess station. It was a large still life of a half-full martini glass with a half-eaten green olive on a toothpick. The piece wasn't for sale – Noam had given it as a thank-you gift for always squeezing him in when, like tonight, the place was overbooked – but its presence there had generated several other sales from art enthusiasts. When he'd walked into Dallal with Chelsea that evening, she spotted the painting and knew instantly that it was one of his. When he confirmed her guess, she beamed with the pride of a game show contestant who'd nailed the winning answer. Inwardly, he'd beamed too. This woman, a stranger with whom he'd spent a matter of hours, somehow *knew* him. Over dinner, they'd talked more about his journey as a hobbyist painter and she asked about his studio set-up. It was then that he offered to show it to her, the extra bedroom in his condo a few blocks away. She'd immediately averted his gaze by looking down at her plate of fish shwarma, and Noam feared that he'd been too forward. He was attracted to her, *very* attracted to her, but he had no plans to try to seduce her, as tempting as it was. She surprised him by replying with a mischievous turn of her full lips, "Why not? I've already blown off a whole day with my tour group. Why stop now?"

"You sure? I know we hardly know each other."

"That's true. But I'm a big girl. And I don't know why but I trust you. If I didn't, I wouldn't have gotten in your car this morning."

At his apartment, she gently flipped through canvases leaned against the wall in his living room. Her fingers were thin and long, with long nail beds but short nails. They were delicate hands, unlike the workhorse hands of other women he'd known – his mother's, his sister's, his friends', his army companions'. Like her chipped front tooth he fixated on, her hands were an odd trait to notice, Noam knew. But that was just it with her: he was drawn to her in odd, unexplainable ways.

"Really, incredible," Chelsea repeated, lifting a medium-sized canvas from the stack. "I especially love this one." It was one of his recent favorites too, a coffee mug resting on top of the front page of the *Jerusalem Post*.

"Thanks. Doing the newspaper...what's that called in English? The newspaper words?"

"Typeface?"

"Yes, doing the typeface was a chore."

Chelsea shook her head in admiration, sliding the painting back to its spot among the others. "I can't even imagine. It looks like a photograph."

How could she know that was the comment he always strived for? He was a realist. He wanted the viewer to pause, forced to wonder whether the image was a photo or a painting.

"Would you like something to eat or drink?" he offered.

"We just had dinner...."

He shook his head and rolled his eyes at himself. *What a dumb thing to –*

"I'd actually love something," she said, her eyes smiling. "I don't know what it is but jet lag hits me in a weird way. My sleep adjusted instantaneously, but I'm hungry all the time."

Noam nodded and spun away from her. *Sleep.* The mention of it filled him with dread. He'd planned to take Chelsea to Independence Hall, drop her back at her hotel and then paint the rest of the day, hoping the tedious work of capturing every shadow, refining every line would trigger an exhaustion greater than his fears. But the day hadn't gone as planned. Her presence here, as pleasant as it was, would require much more mental work later tonight.

"What would you like?" he called to her from the kitchen.

"Water, please. And do you have any Israeli...junk food?"

Noam leaned around the wall of the kitchen to reply. "Junk food?"

Chelsea walked toward him, slipping her wispy honey hair into a low pony tail. "Junk food? It's like food that's not healthy–"

He held up a hand. "I told you, my mom's from Texas. I *know* what junk food is!"

She laughed. "Ouch. Glad I'm not from Texas or I might take that personally."

He smiled then rolled his arm in circles, urging her to explain.

"I haven't traveled a lot. I've barely been out of Colorado. I had one friend growing up who was Korean. Her relatives would always bring her Korean candy and junk food when they visited. The most delicious stuff. From then on I told myself that I'd try junk food in every exotic place I visited. So it's on my personal bucket list for this trip: try Israeli junk food. I was planning to ask my guide once I got to know her a bit. You seem like a pretty...healthy...guy," she said, glancing away from him and blushing a bit. "But I've now seen your paintings of candy wrappers and bags of what look like chips. So I'm thinking you might have some Middle Eastern junk food around here."

Noam gave her a thumbs up and then raised an index finger to indicate he'd return. "Please, sit down," he called from the kitchen. Moments later, he brought her water, a bag of Bamba and a large bar of chocolate laced with Pop Rocks. Her eyes watered upon tasting the chocolate and then experiencing the unexpected explosions in her mouth. And when she tried Bamba, the snack that was like peanut butter Cheetos, she moaned.

"Peanut butter is my desert island food," she said blissfully.

He raised his eyebrows in question.

"Sorry, it's a thing in my family. Desert island food. If you were stranded on a desert island and could have just one food for the rest of your life, what would it be? For me: peanut butter."

"Ahhhh. I'd pick...figs. But I thought you'd pick cinnamon hard candy. I spotted you popping a few of those in your mouth today."

Her face darkened towards the color of the hard candy itself. "Sorry. It's a habit, a bit of an addiction. I know it bugs some people, the sharp smell, the crunching."

"I didn't mind, I just noticed," he said. "Anyway, if you tell my mother I keep this junk here, we're through."

She laughed. Then for the first time since they drove to Independence Hall that morning, they were silent. He took a sip of water. Though he gazed down at his lap, he managed to regard her nonetheless. She was so out of place in his apartment – with her long, thin limbs, her wispy honey hair, her Colorado background, her Christian faith. He was used to Israeli women – feminine, yes, but strong. Army strong. Chelsea seemed delicate – everything from her figure to her manner. At the same time, though, Noam thought she somehow fit. It was like a new piece of furniture or artwork that you placed or hung and needed to get used to. But once you did, you couldn't imagine the room without it. Involuntarily, he shook his head at the image.

"What?" she asked.

"I was thinking how I just don't know anyone like you."

She pursed her lips. "Didn't you say your mother was American?"

"Yes. But she's still a Jew."

"I see."

"Sorry – of course I don't mean that in any bad way. I know from my American cousins that we Israelis can be...abrupt. It's not meant to offend. It's who we are."

"I'm still trying to figure that out. Who are you, exactly? I mean, I still don't get what exactly it means to be Jewish. You're not like those old men on the bus. You said you're not even religious. But you're still Jewish. I don't get it."

He thought about how he'd planned to paint this evening. He had a computer cord all ready to be sketched out, its twists and turns waiting to be shadowed and contoured, and the exercise would be a pathway to the bone-crushing fatigue that he craved. He could smell the damp paint brushes drying in the next room.

She pressed. "How can you be a Jew if you don't practice Judaism?"

"How can I not be?"

She shook her head. "I don't understand."

The canvas, his paints, the twisted cord called to him. He sighed. "Despite what you might think being in this Jewish country – the world's *only* Jewish country – there really are few Jews left. Around the world, since the beginning of time, people try to erase our history. Millions and millions of Jews were systematically murdered less than seventy years ago. My grandmother always implored me – *implore*, is that the word?"

Chelsea nodded, her eyes steady.

"Implored me to never forget. Do you know that if a moment of silence was held for every victim of the Holocaust we'd be silent for eleven and a half years?"

Her face blanched. "My stars. So you're Jewish because you lost family in the Holocaust?"

"I actually didn't lose family in the Holocaust. My mother's parents both came from a long line of only children and they'd all moved to the States or England before the war."

"What about your father's family?"

"My father's family wasn't Jewish."

"But –"

He held up a hand. "My father's family was French-German. My grandfather was an organ player. He made his living playing at religious services throughout Paris, including many synagogues. He fell in love with

Jewish ritual and prayer. He converted, as did my grandmother. My father grew up Jewish after the Holocaust. Although my mom didn't lose family in the Holocaust, growing up in Texas she was asked more than once why she didn't have horns. A swastika was spray painted on her high school to resounding silence from the administration. They didn't even paint over it. She visited Israel as a teenager and made Aliyah right after college."

Chelsea squirreled her eyebrows together.

"Aliyah," Noam explained, "is when a Jewish person moves here. It means immigration to Israel."

"I'm sorry for being pushy, but I still don't understand. You're a Jew who doesn't practice Judaism."

Noam laughed. "Pushy? You're talking to an Israeli. Jews – religious or not – love questions, love debate."

"Good," she said, crunching on Bamba. "Continue."

"I'm a member of a tribe. And what unifies us is not necessarily faith – though many, many Jews are faithful." He took a sip of water. "I'll put it another way. If religion is supposed to be something one believes, then to me, being born into a religion doesn't make sense. That said, I am culturally a Jew because of the customs and manners I was raised with."

"So the Hasidic men on the bus. You don't believe what they believe. We," she waved her hand back and forth between her chest and his, "can touch even though we're not married."

He nodded and shifted on the couch, willing his body to understand that her words formed a question, not an invitation.

"So you helped prevent me from violating a law that you don't even believe in."

"I don't believe. To me, religion is too often a crutch. But I *respect*. Orthodox Jews, Muslims, Christians, Atheists."

"Do you believe in God?"

He exhaled. "I want to...."

She waited.

"I want to. But I just can't. I have no evidence."

"But there's evidence all around!" She declared, sitting up, her eyes shining. "The sea outside my hotel. The fact that your country was even founded – that it still exists. Your very tour today showed that's all the work of His hand."

"No. That's the work of hardscrabble men and women. The result of years of Zionist planning, of men and women risking everything so Jews could return to their homeland. And the sea? That's just the result of millions of years of tectonic plates shifting."

Outside, the sounds of dinner-goers and bar hoppers swelled.

Chelsea shook her head in protest. "Not millions of years...."

"Don't tell me –"

"I'm a Christian," she interrupted, defiant. "I believe in Creationism. I will not apologize."

Noam held up a hand. "Fair enough. Like I said, I don't believe but I respect. For me, I'm a scientist. I demand evidence. But I would never ask anyone to apologize for their own faith. That's why I'm a Dove."

Earlier that day, after they'd left Independence Hall, he'd explained a fundamental difference among Israelis, as deep – if not deeper – than the divisions between American Democrats and Republicans. Doves, like Noam, wanted peace among people, among nations, between Arabs and Israelis, even at great cost. His whole life he'd watched how religion had torn people apart – Jews and Muslims, Orthodox and secular Jews. Once explained to her, Chelsea had come down firmly in the opposite camp. She was a Hawk – strident on national security, insisting that God gave Jews the rights to this ancient land – all of it – forever.

"Let me ask you something," he said. "You keep saying 'He.' How do you know that God is a man?"

"Your own bible, the Old Testament – the basis of my own – tells me that."

He got up and plugged his phone into a speaker. "When I was growing up, my American mother was a raging Barbra Streisand fan. She played her music constantly. By osmosis, I became a fan too." He lowered his voice and added conspiratorially, "If you tell anyone that I voluntarily listen to Streisand, I will have to take drastic measures."

She laughed. "Duly noted."

"Anyway, there's a song – Stoney End – do you know it?"

Chelsea shook her head.

"There's a line; 'I was raised on the Book of Jesus...'til I read between the lines.'"

"Your point?"

"That the Torah refers to God as a man does not in any way persuade me that God, if he or she even exists, is a man."

"Can you be convinced of anything?" she asked, breaking off another corner of chocolate.

He tapped a few buttons on his phone and African-American gospel music emerged from the speakers. He sat back down next to Chelsea, his eyes peering directly into hers. "I'm convinced of things I experience. And I'm convinced that today I had a wonderful time with you."

She raised her eyes to the ceiling. "This doesn't sound like Barbra Streisand."

"It's not. It's the Mississippi Mass Choir. My mom introduced me to Barbra. My friend introduced me to American gospel. I can feel the faith of these musicians, the way I can feel yours. I don't disparage it. In fact, I envy it. I just can't get there myself. At least, not yet."

"So you're searching?" Hopefulness oozed from her and he had a strong drive not to disappoint.

"I'm Israeli and a Jew by culture. As for philosophy or doctrine, the best description I've found at this point is that I'm a Humanist. I believe in rationalism, science, art and compassion. I believe *people* give meaning to their lives. As for God – what's that expression my mom says? – oh, yes, 'The jury's still out.'"

Again, they were quiet, the swells of gospel music and joyful hand clapping accompanying their individual thoughts. Finally, Chelsea stood. "Noam, I have never met anyone like you."

He rose too. They stood a foot apart and yet also, clearly, a world apart. Still, something unseeable buzzed between them. To him, it felt like electricity. Chelsea, he suspected, might characterize it in more supernatural terms, if she felt it too. It took restraint not to gather her into his arms.

She held out her hand. "I've had the most wonderful day – thank you. It wasn't what I expected for my first days here, but it was still fascinating."

"I'll drive you back to the hotel."

"No –," she said, dismissing him with a shake of her head. "You've done too much already. You gave me, a stranger, your whole day. I saw plenty of taxis outside the restaurant around the corner."

He nodded, surprised and maybe even a tad wounded that she referred to them as strangers. They'd spent the full day together and to him it felt that they were not people who didn't know each other. Weirdly, he felt that somehow they'd never been strangers.

"I'll walk you there and tell the taxi driver where to take you."

A few minutes later, when he returned to his apartment alone, Noam paused in the doorway of his home studio. He longed to paint, to capture reality on a piece of stretched linen, to work his eyes and brain and arms so that he could no longer fight sleep. But he couldn't paint. He couldn't even think. He returned to the living room where he'd just been with Chelsea, feeling both a profound connection and an enormous distance. He plugged his phone back into the speaker and played Barbra Streisand into the night.

Chapter Seven

The shrill hotel phone rang and Chelsea shot straight up. Disoriented, she looked around. White sheets, tan carpet, a slash of heavy sunlight peeping through the thin spread of the mostly closed drapes. It took a good ten seconds for her to remember where, exactly, she was. Once she reclaimed her center, she noted again how soundly she slept in the Middle East, half a world away from Colorado Springs.

She rolled over, slammed an arm across the side table and picked up the receiver. "Hello," she croaked.

"We didn't see you all day yesterday! It's Kathleen, from Christian Holy Land Journeys. Just making sure you'll be joining us today. We've got a terrific day planned, beginning with Monday prayer services in forty-five minutes."

Until recently, Chelsea always took advantage of any opportunity to spend a morning at church. Always – growing up, during college, and in the early years with Austin. *Especially* the early years with Austin. She loved the music, she loved that Christ felt so close – it was never a reach or a struggle to be near him at any prayer service. But most of all, she loved the fellowship. That really was the perfect word for her experience – it was social, a coming together of similar individuals around a shared passion. That's how Chelsea felt about Jesus – passionate. He was everything to her: friend, protector, savior, therapist, father. And never more so than at prayer services. This particular morning, she didn't feel like going to a new church with people she didn't know. That fellowship she loved would be lacking. Yet Christ would be there. And that, she reminded herself in the seconds after Kathleen's words, was why she came on this trip: to reconnect with Christianity. *Your faith can move mountains; your doubt can create them.* It was a favorite quote of her mother, who had the saying framed over the kitchen sink. When she returned home, Chelsea would no doubt have to move mountains, to do things she never expected she'd have to do. So she needed Jesus now.

"Right!" Chelsea said cheerily into the receiver, partly for Kathleen's benefit, and partly to generate her own enthusiasm. "Forty-five minutes. I'll be downstairs."

How she longed to enjoy another leisurely hotel breakfast with the olives, the halva. She wanted to read her book while sipping that Turkish-style coffee. But she also wanted a shower. So she unwrapped one of the protein bars she'd brought from home and got herself ready to rejoin the tour.

St. Peter's Church was in Jaffa, on the southern edge of Tel Aviv. On the bus ride there, she chatted absently with her seat mate, a thirty-something man from Pennsylvania. Compared to Austin, he was edgy. Austin had short, straight blond hair with a crisp side part. This man wore his frizzy brown hair in a ponytail. Austin was a business owner – if working for his father's business qualified – and, more recently, a politician. This man was earning a doctorate in Latin American literature. Given the savage demise of her engagement to Austin, this man – Austin's opposite – might otherwise have intrigued her. But today she wasn't comparing the man to Austin. Instead, inexplicably, Chelsea found herself comparing him to Noam.

The day she'd spent with Noam had been unlike any day she'd ever experienced. She learned fascinating tidbits that she hadn't even realized she wanted to know. Like how in Israel's War of Independence, the Haganah (the Zionist youth underground and the precursor to the Israel Defense Forces) turned the tables in just six weeks, regaining control of much of the territory that had already been slotted to the Jewish state under the United Nations Resolution immediately preceding the war. And how the Palmach, the Haganah's elite fighting force, contributed not just militarily to Israel but almost more so to its culture. The practice of Kumzitz (sitting around a campfire eating and talking), public singing and long walking trips were still favorite activities of modern Israelis, she learned. Hearing what the Haganah fighters had to endure just to secure the land they were rightly given, Chelsea wondered how anyone could be anything *but* a Hawk. Yet Noam himself, the person who'd so proudly introduced her to the history of the state of Israel, was a Dove. To Chelsea, it didn't make sense. But a lot of things about Noam didn't make sense. Like how he could painstakingly recreate the creases of a used candy wrapper on canvas. How he was sometimes abrupt with his words, yet gazed at her with attention that was nothing short of rapt. How he'd been an officer in the army but exuded a preternatural gentleness. How, with his black curly hair and olive skin, his tall build, his Barak Obama smile, he looked nothing like anyone she'd ever met.

Thinking of him then, Chelsea fanned herself.

"It sure is hot here in Israel," the ponytailed man remarked.

She nodded and leaned her head against the back of her seat. "You have no idea."

》》》》》》》》》》》》》

THE PRAYER SERVICE IN THE OUTSKIRTS OF TEL AVIV WAS both wonderfully familiar and, at the same time, a lonely experience. The preacher was a man not unlike Pastor Stanton at Pulpit Springs Church, her congregation in Colorado. Both in their forties, both men spoke loudly and fervently – this man, with a British accent. Today's sermon was about one of her favorite stories: when Jesus fed five thousand people with a mere five loaves of bread and two fish. It always reminded her to trust God with what little she had because he could do miraculous things.

Sitting in St. Peter's, she wondered whether she or Austin would "get" their church back at home now that they'd split. Although it was the congregation she'd grown up at, Austin had swiftly made it his own. In fact, Austin's election to City Council wouldn't have happened without the support of her father and, by extension, Pulpit Springs. She hadn't wanted to face it, but here, a half a world away, she had to: there was no way Austin would leave the congregation. If she wanted her Sunday worship and fellowship to not include Austin, it was Chelsea who'd have to find another church. It wouldn't be easy. She never liked the large mega-churches she'd been to for weddings. And without parents, a partner or small children, it wouldn't be easy to find fellowship in another small congregation. Her own father would likely prefer Austin at Pulpit Springs over her. When the English-accented preacher led them in a slow rendition of Great Is Thy Faithfulness, she finally acknowledged this truth and wept.

After the service, the tourists of Christian Holy Land Journeys had lunch at an Italian restaurant. Why Italian food in the Middle East? she wondered, somewhat disappointed. On this trip, she sought authenticity, not ease or familiarity. She wanted to eat Israeli food in Israel. Like the lamb meatballs and roasted root vegetables she'd had for lunch the day before with Noam. Yet the first bite of her wood-fired mushroom pizza changed her judgment – its thin crackly crust and intense fresh tomato flavor made it easily the best pizza she'd ever eaten.

"Wow," she said to nobody in particular, covering her mouth with her hand while she chewed. "Wow."

"I've been to this country three times," said a heavy-set woman in her sixties sitting next to her. "And I've been all over the world. People don't know: the food here is like nothing else. Even Italian food in Israel is better than the Italian food in Italy."

Chelsea nodded enthusiastically and took another large bite.

"'For He satisfies the thirsty and fills the hungry with good things,'" the woman added, winking. "Jesus was Israeli."

"Amen," Chelsea replied.

》》》》》》》》》》》》》》》》》》》

PER THE ITINERARY, THE AFTERNOON WAS FREE, WITH AN option to shop in Tel Aviv's Gan Ha'ir outdoor mall. Chelsea opted to go, inhaling large sniffs of sea air each time she exited a shop. She bought souvenirs for Baylee and her mom, including a small musical nativity scene made mostly of carved wood. She treated herself to ice cream in a waffle cone, its yeasty scent too alluring to resist. By the time dinner rolled around, she was still full and decided to skip the tour's scheduled meal, which was just a buffet in the hotel anyway. She'd hardly spoken with her tour mates, let alone bonded with anyone. She reminded herself that was never the goal of this journey anyway. The one relationship she sought to strengthen here was that with Jesus Christ. As much as she'd spent her life loving him for being her savior, lately she'd felt let down, confused, uncertain of the path he'd put her on. She sought to be reminded of his sovereignty, and retracing his life here was her way of making that happen.

No doubt, her encounters with Noam had further isolated her from the group. Not only had she missed a full day of the trip, but today she felt distracted and daydreamy. They – fellow Americans, Christians – were familiar and, as a result, uninteresting. But Noam was...different, exotic. Magnetic.

She settled into her hotel room for the night, changing into sweats, laying out clothes for the next morning and finding secure spots in her luggage for her new purchases. For company, she turned on the TV.

Although CNN was the obvious choice for an American traveling abroad, she flipped channels, landing on what looked like a prime time soap opera. She couldn't understand the Hebrew but sat on the edge of the bed, riveted nonetheless. Admittedly, she wasn't well-traveled. But in her first few days in Israel, she determined that Israelis had to be the best looking people of any country anywhere. Maybe it was the intense sun. Or the refreshing ocean breezes. Or the conscripted army, which kept everyone healthy and fit. They had bold features and thick hair, blond, black and everything in between. One woman on the soap opera was tall and elegant, her breasts full and high in a sleek evening gown. Noam probably had women like this falling at his feet, she thought, and then switched the TV off, feeling foolish.

She got under the covers and jotted down a few reflections on the prayer service in her navy notebook. Then pulled out *Eat Pray Love*. The author had finished her spiritual search at the ashram and had begun her days in Bali. How her grandmother always knew precisely what book Chelsea needed was a mystery.

Twenty minutes later, as her eyes grew droopy, her cell phone rang.

"Hi, Mama," she answered.

"Honey!" It was clear from the whooshing background noise that she was calling from the car. "We're on our way to a community breakfast at Pulpit Springs. We miss you."

Chelsea's heart hurt. She'd gone on this trip because she need to get away – from home, from everything she'd known – but her mother's voice made her homesick.

"Miss you too."

"What's it like there?"

"It's...different. It's beautiful and fascinating and...confusing."

"How are the people in your group?"

"They're nice enough. I don't really know them. I made one friend." Instantly, she regretted the disclosure.

"Oh? Who is she?"

Chelsea paused. Even as a teenager, she could never lie to her mother. "He. And he's not on my tour. He's an Israeli local I met the first day, before the tour began."

"A Jewish man?"

"He's Israeli. And, yes, he's Jewish. But he's not really...observant."

"Not sure how I feel about either of those facts."

Her voice gathered speed. "He's a painter. And a scientist. Did you know that Israel has the greatest number of scientists and technicians in the world, even more than Japan or Germany?"

"You know, Chelsea, it's the Jews who follow Jesus that are the *real* chosen ones."

Chelsea heard her father speaking in the background. She glanced at the time. She could picture it – they were pulling up to Pulpit Springs, her father rolling down the window to wave and bark greetings to fellow congregants as he parked. It was the same every time. That's what she loved about life there, at least that's what she'd always thought. But like Austin, her father had shocked her, making her question everything she thought she knew.

"Daddy says hi. He's just parking." Her mother had always covered for her father, blanketed his distance with her love so it would be less noticeable. That truth had begun to emerge as Chelsea observed her mother's passive complicity in what Austin and her father had done. Some edges could not be smoothed over with kindness or excuses.

"I know," Chelsea said, suddenly lonesome for home and at the same time relieved she wasn't there. It was a push-pull – the allure of newness, the surety of home. But home, she knew, would never be the same.

"I admire you for walking Jesus's path. Remember, your faith can move mountains...."

Her eyes closed, Chelsea could picture the magnificent, jagged Colorado Rockies her mother was beneath at that moment. She longed for them, yet resented this distraction. She had to spend these weeks shoring up her faith so she could uncover how to best move forward when she returned. This call from home wasn't helping and, if she was honest with herself, neither was the time she'd spent with Noam.

She sighed, "Yes, Mama."

Chapter Eight

noam and Adi had been together for seven months when his army reserve duty approached.

"I can't believe I won't see you for nearly two months," Adi said, sitting cross-legged on his bed wearing one of his sweatshirts and gazing at him from behind her large glasses. He was rolling up t-shirts and shorts and stuffing them into his duffle bag. Though his reserve duty was twenty-five days, her own reserve service would begin three days before his ended, preventing them from seeing each other even for a day in between. As reservists, she updated her code-decrypting skills in the south near Eilat, while as a squad leader Noam split his time between the West Bank and Akko on the coast.

Noam grabbed his travel backgammon set from the drawer of his nightstand – he kept it there because sometimes he and Adi played when they first woke up – and kissed the top of Adi's head, which was covered with thick blond hair.

For millennia, Jews have been targets of elimination. The only thing that changes is the aggressor: Egyptians, Greeks, Romans, Nazis, Arabs. A country that's never had permanent borders, Israel designed its military to match that precarious reality. Service is conscripted, even for women, and the IDF's real strength lies in the miluim, the country's nearly half-million reserve soldiers. Like all Israelis, Noam and Adi accepted this, but it didn't make being separated from a love any easier.

The next morning, after making love and playing a few rounds of rummy (because the backgammon set had been packed away), they said goodbye. Adi handed him a sealed letter he was to read on the bus. He squeezed his eyes shut and shook his head. "Unbelievable," he said, as he reached into his back pocket and pulled out an envelope for her. On the front, it read, "For Adi – to read after my bus drives off."

Once at the base, it took mere hours for Noam to resume the camaraderie with army friends he'd known for a decade. That first night, they teased each other about all the old things: Itai's receding hairline, Moshe's allegedly crooked penis. Pictures were shared of girlfriends, new and old, and in some cases of babies. Instead of missing Adi, Noam in those moments felt a pleasant security in his relationship with her.

It was after returning to regular life while she was on duty that the separation began to torture him. No longer distracted by army duties like operating and fixing machinery or learning the latest artillery, Noam discovered that life in Tel Aviv was now lonely and boring without Adi. Fixating on his reunion with her, he made constant calculations in his head ("sixteen days – that's only twenty-three thousand minutes," he'd reason) and soon had trouble sleeping.

Finally, her duty ended and Noam thought he'd explode with joy when he saw her again. But that first night, at dinner at their favorite Ethiopian food restaurant, Adi was unusually quiet, smiling half smiles instead of the broad one he loved so much. And she was curt in responding to the questions that he'd saved up over the last several weeks. Even though they hadn't been intimate for nearly two months, Adi said she was too tired that night. Next to her, he tossed and turned, terrified that she'd met someone new. She slept soundly, snoring like a buzz saw. In the morning, she reached for him, threading her fingers through his just like she always had.

"I'm sorry," she said, squeezing his hand, shifting her body closer to his and kissing his ear. "I guess I'm like an astronaut. I just need a little re-entry adjustment time."

Another year like that – of consecutive reserve duties – went by, accompanied by that same awkward readjustment that resulted from such a long separation. In plotting his marriage proposal, Noam rolled up the letter granting his request to fulfill his reserve duty the exact same weeks as Adi's and slipped it through the engagement ring that his sister Ronit had helped him pick out.

Adi was murdered before Noam proposed, and the paper and diamond duo remained in the back of his nightstand drawer.

》》》》》》》》》》》》》》》》》》》

AFTER SPENDING THE ENTIRE PREVIOUS DAY WITH CHELSEA, Noam's cranium felt assaulted the moment he arrived at work. The deep orange paint on the walls, the reflection of the metal air ducts, the aroma of air conditioning mixed with the fresh Madonna lilies in a vase at the reception area. Statyst was in a funky warehouse in Azrieli Center, a section of Tel Aviv that had been blooming start ups since the new millennium. Noam had joined the company after completing his army service and earning a degree in statistics. He was Statyst's chief biostatistician, analyzing data related to gangliosides and their role in Alzheimer's and Parkinson's. For the most part, Noam loved the job – it appealed to his orderly brain and he felt good about the company's mission. Plus, the commute was reasonable, many coworkers had become his friends, and the predictable work hours enabled him to spend nights and weekends painting.

"Boker tov," said Gil, a colleague who'd joined Statyst the same month Noam had. Gil had grown up modern orthodox in Haifa but came out as gay after the army. He was still reconciling his observant beliefs with his own biology. Noam joked that Gil was also working his way through a top secret list of gay bachelors in Tel Aviv – as Noam's Texas-raised mother would say, Gil was quite randy. "You look terrible."

"If that's how you pick up men, no wonder you're still single," Noam replied, tossing his backpack on his desk and sinking heavy into his vinyl chair, which expelled a brief whoosh of trapped air. Gil approached him with an expression of concern.

"Didn't sleep, huh?" he whispered.

Gil was one of the few people who knew Noam's private paradox, something he kept secret from most. What kind of sgan aluf – *senior officer* – had this kind of phobia? Snakes was one thing, but this.... Noam loved Gil, loved his work, but at that moment he longed to just spend the day creating in his studio. Painting made him both pleasantly exhausted and electrified. In his studio, he buzzed with visions and a palpable urge to bring them to life with colors and shapes, with his eyes and his hands. Or maybe today he was longing for something else entirely.

Noam shook his head, rubbing his palms vigorously up and down his face. "But not for the usual reason."

Gil raised an eyebrow, conveying, "Do tell."

"I met a woman this weekend –"

Gil snorted. He frequently detailed his own escapades to Noam, but had little patience for stories of traditional male-female hook-ups.

"No," Noam continued. "It's not like that. I mean...." He thought about Chelsea's slim figure, her delicate hands, her oval eyes outlined in too much black liner, her straight hair as flat as the computer screen on his desk, the cross around her neck, the way she said "y'all" when she referred to Jews or Israelis, the way she cocked her head when she twirled the new stud in her upper ear. Maybe most of all, he thought of the way she spoke about God. It was hard to explain, maybe even unexplainable. "Forget it...."

Gil sat on the edge of Noam's desk. "Sorry. That wasn't very empathetic with me." Gil was seeing a new therapist and had recently begun using terms like empathy, resistance, curiosity and acceptance. "Where'd you meet her? Online on Alpha? Dancing at Kuli Alma? Or did your mom set you up again?"

Noam was silent, taking a moment to evaluate whether it was worth the energy to try to explain why this woman – a foreigner, a religious Christian – had lodged in his brain like lyrics from an American one-hit-wonder from the eighties. He decided to give an abbreviated version, partly because he was tired, partly because he wanted to simply gauge Gil's reaction. Speaking about her to a friend might even dissipate the unexpected power she was having over him.

"Her name is Chelsea and –"

Gil widened his eyes and then looked sideways in a dramatic, comical fashion.

Noam sat up. "Right. American. Not Jewish. Not just not Jewish but Christian. *Very* Christian. She's here on a Jesus tour. Wears a cross – a *cross*. I met her on the Efal Street bus Friday night when she was about to sit next to some Haredim."

Gil snorted, then smiled. "So you rescued her?"

"Or them, depending on how you look at it. Anyway, I ran into her again the next day and we spent the day together on Sunday."

Gil leaned forward.

Noam headed off his friend's probe. "Nothing happened. But...."

"You wanted to? With a goyim? A shiksa? And I thought it was hard to come out as gay."

"Well," Noam said, "as you know, my family, unlike yours, is not religious. So I'm not exactly sure how they'd respond. And anyway, what difference does it make? I don't even know the woman. She's here for like a month or two and then returns to the Wild, Wild West. I'll never see her again." His voice caught, which surprised him. He coughed exaggeratedly in an attempt to cover it up. "She just stirred up something in my brain."

"Stirred up something in your *brain*, huh?" Gil said. Then his voice got low. "The last time you described a woman that way, you'd just met Adi."

A realist and a skeptic, Noam didn't believe in things he couldn't see, things that couldn't be objectively verified, whether it was God or the notion of having one true soul mate. But had he been open to the concept of something like that or in love at first sight, Adi would have been Exhibit A. He'd met her five years before and was struck instantly by her thick blond hair, her wide smile, her black eye glasses that were sexy in their nerdiness. Adi was the most compassionate person he'd ever met, a skill she'd honed as a peer counselor in the army. When Noam met her, she was studying Russian literature at Haifa University. They dated for nearly two years and just as Noam was working up the nerve to propose, she was blown up by a suicide bomber who pulled a cord on his vest in a cafe a few miles outside Ramallah.

"Thanks, Gil," Noam said, feeling slightly sick at the memory of the most profound love – and grief – he'd ever felt. "Helping to start my day off right...."

Gil held up his palms and then wagged a finger. "Sorry, *buuuut* I'm making a point here. I know you, Noam. There's something different about this shiksa you just met. Deny it all you want, but I have x-ray vision when it comes to love."

Noam rolled his eyes and sighed. "Can we start this day all over again?"

"Seriously. Do not ignore your feelings here. Do you have a picture of her?"

"Why would I have a *picture* of her? I hardly know the woman."

"No selfies during your day together?"

Noam recalled their escapades through Tel Aviv – museums, cafes, art galleries, dinner at Dallal, the junk food at his apartment – nothing touristy that was suitable for selfies. Most prominently, he recalled their conversations – actually, it was more like a single, twelve-hour conversation because they barely stopped talking. They spoke about the political and religious forces that led to the founding of Israel, about Noam's being both an army officer and a Dove, what Colorado was like, music and books, and, most interesting to Noam, they spoke about faith. He admitted to being both jealous and skeptical of hers, even as she admitted to being in the midst of a faith crisis herself, which is what brought her to Israel. When she described finding Christian Holy Land Journeys as "a God miracle," he'd responded, with true curiosity, "How do you know it was God? Wasn't it just...a coincidence? Or a lucky break?" She'd paused, gazing at him with warmth and maybe a bit of pity, "How do you know it *wasn't* God?" He'd had no answer.

"Nope, no picture of her. She's pretty," he said, remembering how many times he suppressed the urge to touch her, to lift with his fingers loose hair that had slipped from her pony tail, to kiss her. "She's petite. She has light brown hair, big eyes. White teeth with one crooked and chipped. She wears too much makeup and a cross. But she's beautiful and different. And she's...anyway, I've just never met anyone like her."

Later that day, long after his conversation with Gil, the day he'd spent with Chelsea lodged sideways in his brain as he reviewed quantitative analyses of isolated gangliosides in mice. Then he roamed, as he sometimes did, to the company's on-site lab, and gazed through the glass into the hermetically sealed room. He observed other kinds of scientists – those in crisp, white lab coats and hair nets – dance between microscopes and computers, between freezers and neat rows of test tubes.

Did these people believe in God? Noam wondered. The logic of the scientific world clashed against odd twinges in his heart. Chelsea's faith drew out his scientist's curiosity. Despite himself, something about her made him eager to test the untestable, to look for the unseeable.

Chapter Nine

The night before her last morning in Tel Aviv, Chelsea slept hard. Her dreams were varied, but intense. Right before her alarm sounded was the most intense dream of all. She was in Noam's apartment, sitting on the couch next to him just like she had the other night. In the dream, a purple-ish current – visible to the naked eye – linked them. His blue eyes bored into hers and she didn't look away. Instead, she was propelled by an invisible force. She moved her body closer to his, a small shift at first. In response, he remained motionless, looking not just at her but *into* her. She moved closer, again and again until she was so close she could see the red veins in his eyeballs. Still, he didn't move, though the corners of his lips curled by millimeters upward. Eventually, he leaned back, not a move away from her, but an invitation. She got closer, the tips of their noses touching. She could smell him, his pheromones, and the purple current hummed. Then her alarm buzzed and she abruptly woke, panting and with drool drizzled on her pillow.

She rolled onto her back and threw her forearm over her eyes, working to bring the pace of her breath back to normal. Then she glanced to the left, to the empty spot in the bed next to her. The dream had felt so real, she had to double check that Noam wasn't actually lying beside her. She could still feel his presence. She knew it was crazy but she wondered if somehow he had dreamt the same dream. To her, it felt like a message of some kind, maybe from Noam. Maybe from God.

She looked to the right to view the time. She had a few minutes before she had to get ready and pack up for breakfast and checkout. She grabbed her phone and scrolled through the many messages that had come in while her whole community had been going about their day on the other side of the earth. Baylee reported from Guatemala that the mission was going smoothly and she'd become addicted to rice, beans and plantains for breakfast. Chelsea's best friend Crystal sent a video of her toddler daughter. "Look what she learned in VBS!" Crystal wrote. The video was shot from the front seat of Crystal's minivan, looking into the second row, where her daughter, complete with bed head and a plastic container of goldfish crackers, belted out a dramatic rendition of "Jesus Loves Me." At the conclusion, the frame jiggled as Crystal clapped, then she aimed the camera on herself, asking, "Chels, isn't that the most precious thing you've ever seen? I thought you'd especially like it since we met in Vacation Bible School the summer before kindergarten. Miss you."

Seeing Crystal's face filled Chelsea with homesickness – not just for Colorado Springs or her best friend but for the life she'd given up. Like the best friends they were, they'd had it all planned. Chelsea was to get pregnant on her honeymoon with Austin, and Crystal would time her second pregnancy as close to that as she could. They'd even plotted out homeschooling together. Maybe one of them would have a boy and one would have a girl and they'd grow up together and fall in love, meaning that after decades of friendship Crystal and Chelsea would really become family. But Chelsea had destroyed that dream. Even though it was Austin who'd acted in unchristian ways, no one else seemed to view their split as his fault.

Watching the video from a Hyatt hotel in Tel Aviv, Chelsea saw in 3D the life she was supposed to have and how far away it really was. Part of her still wanted it – the simplicity of that life, the sameness, the predict-ability. She knew the schools her kids would attend because she'd gone to them herself. She knew where she'd spent every Sunday for the rest of her life. She knew the neighborhood they'd live in, the friends she'd keep, the luxuries they could afford. She knew the songs she'd listen to, the vaca-tions they'd go on. And that, she'd come to realize, was what had appealed to her about marrying Austin. She was slowly coming to admit that she'd never been passionate about him. Ever. What she'd been passionate about was the life promised by becoming his wife. For that, she felt a mix of uncomfortable emotions – guilt, shame – and now, with the demise of that life, terror. And yet she was also beginning to wonder what he'd truly felt about her. When he knelt on one knee holding a black engagement ring box, his proposal began, "Next to my faith, you are the most important thing to me." Instinctively, she'd felt stung by the remark – *next to* my faith – but then told herself to feel gratitude for finding such a Godly man.

Now, Colorado Springs was Austin's. The life Chelsea had planned seemed impossible. What came next was up to God. And getting some reassurance that God could be trusted again was what brought her to this bed in a Tel Aviv hotel, where she'd awakened panting from a dream about a blue-eyed Jewish man.

In the lobby, she dropped her bags among the group's pile. The tour agenda called for breakfast bible study in a lower-level conference room. This morning's passage was Jeremiah Twenty-nine Eleven: "'For I know the plans I have for you,' declares the Lord, 'plans to prosper you and not to harm you, plans to give you hope and a future.'"

She stood in the lobby observing her tour mates – the sweet, elderly couple from New Jersey, the British family with three young children, the post-college sisters from Atlanta. They were all lovely people, fellow Christians eager to explore Jesus's path just like her. In one way or another, they'd fit well into Pulpit Springs. It was fellowship with people just like this that Chelsea loved so much about her church. But the dream of Noam still covered her, like a thick fog. It felt like a message.

Quickly, she found Kathleen, the tour leader, and asked about the scheduled departure time to the Dead Sea. They'd be leaving in just over an hour.

"Are you sure you want to miss another bible study? This is Jeremiah Twenty-nine Eleven, a popular but often misunderstood verse," Kathleen asked.

Chelsea responded, partly to appease the leader, partly to reassure herself of her commitment to Jesus. "Yes, that passage is not about escaping a bad fate, but about learning to thrive despite it. It's one of my favorites."

Outside the Hyatt, she sucked in the dry heat and gazed at the Mediterranean. Without the protective cover of the Colorado Rockies, the world felt especially large. She spun around and headed towards the Nehama cafe. Foot traffic was lighter than it had been the first time she'd found herself there and Chelsea realized it was a regular day in Tel Aviv. No Shabbat. Most locals, including Noam, were probably at work. Where was his office? she wondered, realizing she knew little about him. Yet part of his mystery and allure was how familiar he felt. And though they'd not spoken in her dream, its intensity somehow made her feel that she now knew him even better. The dream was so acute that she felt with a weird certainty that he'd had the same dream, that he'd know to be the Nehama cafe too. As she marched down the street in a tank top and flip flops, she felt hot air on her skin, similar to the way his body heat had felt in her dream as she'd inched closer and closer to him. She brought a hand to her face to cool herself, to prove that she was now awake.

So consumed by thoughts of Noam, she walked right past Nehama. Standing on the corner, she spun around. Apple store. Arab bakery. Book store. Not-yet-open ice cream store. A group of black-hatted religious men smoking on the corner. Finally, she got her bearings and backtracked down the same block, shaking her head at her distractedness. Once inside, she stood still. At the window table she'd occupied the other day sat another woman. A different barista – a dark-skinned man with dreadlocks to his waist – was behind the counter. Two little boys wearing head coverings squealed as they chased each other around the empty tables upstairs. Wake Me Up Before You Go-Go played on the speakers.

"Ath btvr?"a man behind her said.

Confused, Chelsea turned. Realizing the man was speaking to her, she very nearly responded, "No hablo espanol" before he added in jagged English, "Are you in line?"

She stepped aside with a defeated half-smile.

What was she doing here? She should be discussing Jeremiah Twenty-nine Eleven. She felt utterly ridiculous. Did she think that she was living in some fantastical romcom? That Noam had the exact same dream as her, that it was some kind of secret message to meet again at this spot? It was absurd. The dream was merely a dream, a patently obvious expression of pent-up hormones, nothing more. After all, Austin had insisted that they stop sleeping together once they got engaged. They'd been sexually intimate since soon after meeting and they lived together for years. But once they were officially to be married, he wanted to be "pure before God," insisting that they not have sex again until they were married. Standing alone in that Israeli cafe, Chelsea realized Austin's bizarre hypocrisy was a harbinger of what had been to come.

She slumped into a nearby chair. "Jesus, Jesus, please help me," she whispered, lowering her head and digging the heels of her hands into her eye sockets.

Moments later, her phone beeped, alerting her that she had twenty minutes to return to the hotel for the drive to the Dead Sea. The lowest place on earth. How fitting.

She'd be leaving Tel Aviv, the city whose name meant "old new land," according to Noam. Chelsea, too, was caught between old and new.

What did she still want from her old life? And what "new" could possibly be out there for her? It was for Christ to determine. And clearly, he was already showing her that Noam was just a blip, something to remember about this journey, but not someone to take with her.

She looked up and spotted the wall of Noam's paintings. She crossed the cafe and gazed at the collection up close. They were colorful and pains-takingly realistic. A small painting that she hadn't noticed the other day – no more than seven inches square – caught her eye. It was a collection of Tel Aviv street signs – in English, Arabic and Hebrew. She wasn't familiar with the street – Begin Road – but she didn't care. The shades of blue, purple and white were striking and calming, and the image felt very, very Israeli, the perfect way to commemorate her first days in the Holy Land.

A server walked by and Chelsea asked her to translate the price tag, which was in Hebrew. It would represent a large portion of her spend-ing money for the whole trip, and she still had weeks to go. What other treasures would she find here that she'd want to bring back to Colorado? Money would be so tight when she returned. And yet she didn't care. She had to trust in God, who'd brought her to this cafe, who showed her the wall of Noam's artwork when she looked up from her plea. She bought the painting and carried it back to the Hyatt between two sheets of brown butcher paper. As she walked, the dream slid to the back of her mind, a slightly embarrassing, fading memory. As she recommitted to her Holy Land journey, she said softly, her words swept up by a sea breeze, "Thank you, Jesus."

Chapter Ten

I must be insane, Noam thought as he drove to his parents' house in Tel Aviv's Old North neighborhood. He couldn't sleep – that was nothing new. But now he couldn't paint or even think. A week ago his life was plodding along as normal – maybe a little predictably, but he liked it that way. Then he met a shiksa on the Efal Street bus, spent a grand total of twelve hours with her and now felt as if he couldn't plant his feet on the ground. An American tourist had somehow unmoored him, and he couldn't figure out why.

Sure, she was beautiful – the almond-shaped eyes, the silky thin hair, her delicate frame, that one crooked tooth. Something about that tooth killed him. But she also wore too much makeup and, of course, the prominent cross. That it was a cross was only part of the problem. A Hamsa, a Chai or Star of David necklace also have rubbed Noam, who was decidedly secular, the wrong way. Admittedly, he'd begun spiritually searching a little, reading books about Buddhism, for example. And he'd confess to anyone that he was jealous of the comfort she obviously found in her faith. But although Noam was willing to be convinced of the divine, God, some higher power, he never was. His sister Ronit had tried to explain her own nearly militant devotion to Hashem, but he couldn't buy into it. Chelsea similarly explained that when she considered finger-prints and DNA, the way a baby is designed and grows in the womb, or photosynthesis, she knew – just *knew* – that she had been created. "That," Noam had responded, "is pure biology." Chelsea looked hurt – her expression not unlike Ronit's when they'd had the same discussion – and Noam was tempted to apologize. But he couldn't bring himself to apologize for a statement that to him was as patently true as the fact that his name was Noam.

He pulled up to his parents' home, a contemporary two-story house set back from the street and down a flight of slate stairs, the house they'd moved to from Haifa after Noam and Ronit left home. As he walked down the stairs, he moved aside fronds and large leaves of the plants his mother spent hours cultivating. Inside the front door, he yelled, "Ima, Aba, I'm here." Their language was a mix of Hebrew and English, with splashes of French and Yiddish. His mother had always wanted him to speak English with an American accent ("Just in case," she always said, though Noam never knew exactly what that meant).

"I'm upstairs! Be right down. Aba is coming soon with the food."

"I have the canvases," Noam called up. His mother's best friend had moved to a new condo and wanted "contemporary art" for her walls. She'd purchased a colorful triptych, one of Noam's rare landscapes, from his website.

"Great! You can put them in the DD." Doomsday Den. Bomb shelter. Almost every Israeli homeowner had a bomb shelter. Though it was the tiniest country – no bigger than the state of New Jersey, as Jewish Americans were fond of saying – it had been under threat of attack almost constantly since its founding. Jordan, Egypt, Syria, Hamas, Iran. At one time or another, someone wanted the world's only Jewish state obliterated. Never mind that the world was home to dozens of Arab and Muslim countries. Every Israeli simply lived with the unending threat of bombs, homemade or nuclear. In Israel, gas masks were as omnipresent as toilets.

Instead of making them fearful, it made them defiant and life-loving, characteristics that Noam especially loved about his fellow citizens.

He brought the canvases to the DD then helped himself to what his mom called fancy water. On the kitchen counter, his mom always had a pitcher of water with slices of fruit. Sometimes grapes, sometimes kiwis. Even figs and dates. Today, it was raspberries. Fernando, the family cat, purred as he marched figure eights between Noam's legs.

"Hi, my boy!" his mom said as she came down the stairs. She wore jeans and a V-neck t-shirt.

He leaned down to respond to the arms she held out wide open. She squeezed him too hard, but it felt good to Noam. "Let's sit. Aba is on his way. Ronit is popping by too."

"Why?" The goings on of his sister's life baffled him. After being raised, like Noam, as a secular, nationalistic Jew, she'd become strictly orthodox right after her army service. In the army, she'd met Guy, who, like Ronit, had been raised without much religion. But he began reading about Judaism, something he felt he had to do as an army member charged with protecting the Jewish state, and then attending orthodox services. Ronit followed along and they adopted a wholly orthodox life after the army – so much so that they were excused from sherut milu'im, the reserve duty required after the initial three years of service. They refrained from birth control (hence, Noam's seven nieces and nephews), kept a kosher home (two sets of dishes, two sinks, everything separated between meat and milk), and prayed separately in their synagogue, which they attended every single day. And like the men on the bus, man-woman touching between non-spouses was prohibited. Guy took up studying Torah full time – an admirable vocation among the orthodox – while Ronit supported the family by working long hours as a social worker and raising their seven children.

"She needs to borrow my extra large salad bowl for a dinner she's hosting." Anyone who knew his mom less than Noam would miss that she rolled her eyes just slightly. "As if she doesn't have enough to do...."

Noam's parents silently supported – and silently objected – to Ronit's lifestyle. Their mom had confided in Noam that she believed Ronit turned to orthodoxy because everything (*everything* – from food preparation to sex on Shabbat) was strictly divided – it was either obligatory or forbidden. That kind of life appealed to Ronit, who had long suffered from indecision and an overly deliberative personality. That what she should wear and how she should educate her children were set forth brought her peace. She'd grown humorless since becoming orthodox but also enviably calm despite her harried life. Noam's parents hated how overworked Ronit was – they felt Guy took advantage of her and the centuries-old pronouncements about studying Torah. And more broadly they resented the ultra religious for causing political tensions in Israel's well-planned democracy. But they said nothing, at least not to Ronit. They didn't want to lose her or their grandchildren.

"Thanks for letting me come," Noam said, changing the subject. He'd invited himself to dinner hoping that being with his parents would ground him somehow.

His mom waved a hand as if to say, "Don't be silly." She got up to replenish his fancy water. "So, how are you, my boy?"

"I'm good. Tired." Fernando hopped onto his lap and Noam scratched under his chin.

"Have you seen Doctor Geshen? I told you she's supposed to be the best with phobias."

"Not yet, Ima."

"Oh, you Israelis. With your army service and your toughness. Go. To. A. Doctor. There's nothing to be ashamed of."

"You're Israeli, Ima."

"But I grew up a neurotic American. It's different. Seeing a therapist was de rigeur where I grew up. There's a reason people go. They're helpful."

Shards of late afternoon dark orange light sliced through the blinds, hitting the kitchen table where they rested in lengthy, geometric pillars. His mom noticed too and got up to grab a pad of scratch paper and a pen from her makeshift workspace in the kitchen's corner. Silently, she handed them to Noam, who began to sketch the lines on the table.

"The last week I haven't been sleeping for another reason. I met a woman on the bus."

His mother's face remained neutral, which Noam appreciated. At his age, his friends' mothers were becoming pushy about marriages and babies.

He continued. "She's American."

"American from where?" she asked perkily. Jews were always eager to make connections among the tribe.

"I promise you don't know her or her family. She's from Colorado Springs and she's a Christian, here on a 'Holy Land' tour."

"You're right," his mom sat back against the chair. "I wouldn't know her."

Noam smiled. His doodles went from sharp and linear to loopy and disjointed. "She's here on a spiritual journey. Walking Jesus's path to reconnect with her Christianity. I think she suffered some type of setback or trauma back home."

"How much time did you spend with this woman from the bus?"

"Like a day. I showed her around Tel Aviv a bit. "

"That's not much time. And you can't sleep because of her? She must be a good-looking shiksa."

"It's not that." Despite his words, Noam felt his body stiffen and tingle picturing Chelsea. "I mean, she's pretty. Wears too much makeup. But,

I don't know, we connected. In one weird way, she reminds me of you. She says things like, 'Israel is hotter than a Times Square Rolex.'"

His mother pinched her lips together, trying to stifle a grin of recognition or admiration.

He continued, "And she was fascinated by the national history of Israel – you know, one of my favorite topics. And her faith kind of fascinated me."

His mother stiffened. "Ronit becoming orthodox was one thing. But if you convert –"

Noam held up a hand. "No, no. I don't want to become Christian. But the comfort she takes in her religion...well, it's not unlike Ronit's. As you know, I don't have that comfort."

The pen ran out of ink. He shook it, trying to squeeze some last color out of it.

"Fervent religion has caused many, many problems for our people and others across millennia," his mom said.

"Look who I found outside!" Noam's father announced as he opened the front door carrying a bottle of wine and a bag from their favorite take-out restaurant.

Noam and his mother stood. She kissed his father's cheek and then Noam followed. Ronit came in the door behind their father. She wore her normal garb: a long, dark grey skirt, a long-sleeved black shirt, and a sheitel, the wig covering her natural hair. She was not supposed to touch Noam but it was one of the few proscriptions she ignored. She stood on her tiptoes and hugged him around the neck. She smelled slightly damp with perspiration. It was ninety degrees out at dinner time and she'd been wearing those body coverings and wig all day at the hospital where she was a social worker.

Ronit stayed only a few minutes. They exchanged general pleasantries – How were the kids? What was he painting lately? – and then she was off to cook dinner for her family of nine while her husband stopped at shul on his way home from studying Torah all day. Noam tried not to judge. After all, Ronit had found such solace in her beliefs. Yet he didn't like how paternalistic the orthodoxy was – how unevolved and unbalanced some of the traditions were.

After Ronit left, Noam and his parents enjoyed a low-key meal: rice with roasted vegetables and spices, all so deliciously salty, which they washed down with a glass of white wine from the Golan. They spoke of politics and places they'd take his mom's college roommate from Texas when she came for a visit in December. Noam was thankful his mom didn't resume their conversation about Chelsea. Yet he was also a bit disappointed. He was confused. He needed guidance or clarification. But he hadn't gotten it this evening.

Taking a last sip of wine, he remembered how tired he was. He helped his mother with the dishes and then said his goodbyes, promising to return for another meal before too long. As he climbed the steps to the street, his mother called to him.

"Thought you might want this," she said, handing him the scratch paper with his doodles, the indigo lines giving way to simple paper scratches as the ink ran dry. "For inspiration or something."

"Thanks, Ima." He gave her another tight hug, which, he suspected, was the real reason she came out after him. When he got in the car, he crumpled the paper in his fist and drove away.

Chapter Eleven

hough not strictly a Christian site, the Dead Sea was always included in Christian Holy Land Journeys. It was, as Kathleen declared, "a crowd pleaser." Once she got there herself, Chelsea could see why.

She'd slept on the ninety-minute bus ride from Tel Aviv. She hadn't wanted to – she'd been eager to see the Bedoins with their camels along the desert highway that she'd read about – but the long eastward stretches of road, the rhythmic motion of the bus and the heat combined to make her sleepy. Perhaps I have delayed-onset jet lag, Chelsea thought drowsily as she opened one eye to see more road and sunlight out the bus window. The diagnosis made her smile and she made a mental note to text Baylee about it. But by the time they pulled into Kalia Beach, she was so groggy she couldn't remember what it was that she had told herself to remember.

"Everyone, please leave your belongings on the bus. Just bring your beach bag without valuables. No cash is required either. We've arranged for soft drinks and popsicles in one hour," Kathleen instructed. "Head over to the changing area."

Kalia Beach was an open air attraction of sorts – changing area and showers to the right, two cafes (one outdoor and one indoor) to the left. After Chelsea changed into her bathing suit, a forest green one-piece with thin white diagonal stripes that she rarely got the opportunity to wear in Colorado, she followed the English directions on the wooden signs down the stairs and along paths to the beach itself. She tossed the standard-issue white towel onto a chair near the outdoor showers where several young families were giggling as they wiped thick grey mud off their bodies. Signs by the water warned not to let the Dead Sea water into one's eyes or mouth.

Before stepping out of her flip-flops, Chelsea took a moment to glance across the water to Jordan. It appeared so incredibly close – she believed she could swim there in about a half hour if she were in better shape.

The Dead Sea was the lowest point on the planet, way below sea level and an especially far vertical distance from Chelsea's home in mile-high Colorado. Salt and minerals settled and concentrated in the water causing nothing to live in it and allowing humans to float in it. The sea floor consisted of mud that was said to have healing powers.

Others from her group collected at the shore. Matthew (the name, she'd learned, of the man with the ponytail) was wearing bright red swim shorts. She noted that he seemed to have no hair other than that on his head. Two twenty-something women from her tour approached the sea edge in modest-dress bathing suits that exposed skin only from knees and elbows down.

Though she was at the lowest point on earth, the sun felt close, searing the top of her head. She dipped a toe into the water hoping to cool off but found that it was warmer than bath water. Still, it felt good. She waded in, bending her knees and scooping mud with her hands as she walked deeper into the water.

"Look at me," yelled Matthew, who was lying effortlessly on his back in the water with his hands behind his head as if he were relaxing before a TV in the sky.

Chelsea didn't know if he was talking directly to her or to the heavens. Still, she said, "Cool." Leaning back, she adopted his position and felt herself buoyed up. It was a comforting sensation, being held up by nature.

"Try this," he yelled, this time unquestionably to her. Now, he was upright, looking as if he was standing erect in the water, even though he was far too deep to plant his feet on the sea floor. Chelsea tried it herself and smiled at another marvelous new sensation.

God is so good, she thought as happy teardrops emerged from the sides of her eyes. She used the back of her finger to wipe them away and instantly regretted it. The stinging salt was nearly unbearable. She looked skyward and blinked, letting the scorching sun rays heal her. She made her way to a shallower area and rubbed mud onto her arms, legs and neck. Everything tingled. Maybe it was wishful thinking but it felt healing – not just for her skin, but her soul too. It felt as if what she'd left in Colorado – Austin, her father, the scandal, the loss of the life she'd planned on – existed on another planet. Jordan still felt close, but in that moment the world once again felt very large. She said it once more, this time out loud, "God is good."

〉〉〉〉〉〉〉〉〉〉〉〉〉〉〉〉〉〉〉〉

THAT NIGHT, AFTER AN OUTDOOR "MOONLIGHT PICNIC" consisting of pita bread, minty tabbouleh and the most luscious ice cream sundae Chelsea had ever tasted, she settled into the motel room where she'd sleep just one night before the group traveled to Jerusalem the next morning. She was in a good mood. After the soak in the Dead Sea, her Tel Aviv dalliance seemed farther away than ever, and her faith-based journey was back on track. She was even social during dinner, chatting with Shannon, a fifty-something woman she hadn't met before, about one of the bible's most perplexing proverbs: "The heart of man plans his way, but the Lord establishes his steps." It was a perennial discussion for Chelsea: free will versus God's sovereignty. Shannon was squarely in the God's sovereignty camp, believing that God sees all, controls all, knows all, and that free will is a fiction, something that man just doesn't have. This proved to be an area in which Chelsea could be convinced either way – she saw merit in both sides. "I guess I won't know for sure until I get to Heaven," she commented at the end of her conversation with Shannon, whose smile belied frustration that she hadn't convinced Chelsea of her position. Chelsea pretended not to notice as they departed for their individual rooms, and she noted how Shannon contrasted with Noam, who'd approached their conversations about faith and beliefs with open-mindedness, which was especially remarkable considering how divergent their backgrounds and views were. She shook her head slightly as she walked the outdoor steps to her room, as if to jar his image from between her ears. Maybe Tel Aviv wasn't yet as far away as she'd believed.

After dinner, she took her first proper shower since the Dead Sea, and thin, previously disguised clumps of green-grey mud slid out of her hair and from between her toes. She patted her face with a thick white towel and leaned in towards the mirror, assessing the rejuvenating powers of the sea minerals. Her skin was rosy and plump.

She exchanged texts with Baylee, who reported that she had a crush on a fellow missionary and feared she'd never see him again once their work was done. (Didn't she realize that missions were set up not just to facilitate service work and to share the gospel but to foster romances between like-minded young Christians? Chelsea thought.) Then she sent short messages to Crystal and her mother. To her mom, she ended with the ground-covering "Say hi to everybody," since it would be a long time before Chelsea felt like communicating directly with her father. And she suspected the feeling was mutual.

She cracked open *Eat Pray Love*, skimming back over some of her favorite passages, which she'd underlined. It was a story of someone who felt ruined by trauma and disappointment but then healed through travel, and learned to let go, to move on. It was uncanny how the stories her grandmother chose for her unfailingly fit squarely with what Chelsea needed to learn at that precise moment in her life. It was especially remarkable because her grandmother had been gone for more than five years.

She stayed up past midnight to finish the book and cried at the last line, which was so full of hope, "Attraversiamo – let's cross over."

That's precisely what Chelsea believed this Holy Land trip was to do: help her cross over from past to future.

》》》》》》》》》》》》》》》

THE NEXT MORNING THE GROUP CHECKED OUT EARLY AND had sack breakfasts on the bus as they began the hour-long drive to Jerusalem, a destination for which Chelsea was both excited and nervous. She'd waited her whole life to walk Jesus's Stations of the Cross, but she'd also heard that sharp Arab-Israeli tensions were the most palpable in Jerusalem.

They arrived at the hotel, a small establishment in the Zion Square neighborhood. In the lounge area near reception, Chelsea could have sworn she spotted Noam. Her heart thudding excitedly against her ribs, she moved towards him, only to discover that the tall, dark-haired man with an athletic build was someone else altogether. Up close, he had the same physicality as Noam but none of the magnetism. She immediately felt foolish for hoping it was him, like a dopey teenager who's disappointed when her crush fails to show up at the football game.

Minutes later, when she entered her room to drop off her bags, she discovered a package on the desk. It was from the bookstore that sent books on behalf of her grandmother. It appeared that her mother had forwarded it soon after Chelsea left on the trip. Once again, the timing was miraculous, and Chelsea hoped the story would be as fitting as the last one.

Inside the box was a paperback copy of *Marjorie Morningstar*. Chelsea hadn't heard of it. She scanned the back, learning it was "a feminist saga" about a traditional Jewish girl who attempts to live a life different from the one her parents and community expect.

"Yet again, Granny," Chelsea said out loud, shaking her head in disbelief. "Yet again."

Chapter Twelve

He was supposed to be painting. He'd set aside everything that day: errands, social plans, work reports he needed to catch up on. But rather than painting, Noam sat upright on his couch, his arms spanning its length, staring unfocused at his coffee table, where for the past week he'd been tossing items for potential still lifes: a matchbook from a favorite bar, an empty kombucha bottle, a worn-out phone charger.

Yet...he couldn't paint.

Instead, suddenly energized by a tiny thought that quickly turned into permission, he grabbed his laptop and opened Facebook. Why had he not gotten her number? He typed in Chelsea Brinker. Eighteen entries appeared. His lips turned into an involuntary smile – eighteen entries. That must mean something. Comprised of the Hebrew letters het and yud, eighteen was chai, the word for life, a symbolic number for Jews. Eighteen minutes was the amount of time it took matzo dough to leaven. According to Ronit, God's name is mentioned eighteen times in the shema, the Hebrew prayer that affirms faith in God. That there were eighteen results – Chelsea herself would probably glean some divine significance in that. If she were Jewish....

Noam blinked away the thought and refined his search. He typed, "Chelsea Brinker Colorado."

One hit.

There she was. He clicked her profile and scanned her wall. She didn't post much. She was tagged in photos from a baby shower a few months before. He spotted her instantly amidst the group of excessively blond women. Her smile was warm and tender and in that photo she was not only wearing too much eyeliner but also too much blush and too dark lipstick. She looked distracted in most of the pictures. In one, a group shot of seven women with their arms around each other, she appeared to Noam the most vibrant of the group, as if everyone else had been slightly blurred by the camera's aperture. She glowed. He hit the down arrow, scrolling through more photos. There were pink and blue plastic table coverings, girls wearing plastic baby bellies, plastic trays of food and half-full plastic soda bottles. "Goyish," he could picture his mother saying if she saw the photos. Tacky.

The first real post of hers was a few months old. She'd written: "Jesus was looking out for me this morning! I spent two minutes trying to grab our morning newspaper, which had been tossed into bushes in front of our house instead of on the doorstep as usual. I got mud on my skirt and had to change. By that time, I was running nearly ten minutes late for work and really stressed! Then I discovered there was a six-car pileup on the highway up ahead – exactly where I would have been if I hadn't been running late. Phew! To those who doubt: 'If there's a gift, there must be a giver!'"

If she were beside him, Noam would ask why Jesus hadn't been looking out for the people in the six cars that had been in the accident. He'd ask why didn't it occur to her to simply thank the sloppy newspaper deliverer. Wasn't it that person – that *person* – who'd favorably altered the course of her morning, rather than God? Noam actually wanted to know. And that was the thing about her – he felt that he could ask these questions.

With anyone else, he might be snarky. With anyone else, including his sister, he'd be using the question as a way to make a point. But with Chelsea, Noam truly wanted to discuss this. He hadn't decided – was her faith a weakness? Or maybe that kind of faith gave someone true relief – relief from fear, from guilt, from shame. Would that kind of trust in God have eased his suffering after Adi was killed? Would having that kind of deep, visceral faith enable him to sleep? Even if it could, faith wasn't something you acquired easily. You had to believe it. And belief was something you couldn't force – on yourself or anyone else. Noam had seen too many terrorists try.

Her most recent post, made just nine days ago, was a photo of an orange sun setting behind a mountain. Her caption: "Done."

He clicked "About," hoping she'd listed a phone number in her profile. But like any smart, attractive woman online, she'd left her personal information blank.

Harah. *Shit.*

He considered sending her a Facebook message but from the looks of her account, she didn't log on much. Plus, he didn't want to write to her, he wanted to talk to her, to see her. To hold her. He swung around and grabbed his phone from the side table. He stood and dialed the one person who might have the faintest idea where Chelsea could be. Israel was a small country but she was still among millions. And he didn't even know what city she was in.

"Noam! Achi!" *My brother.*

"Yakov, my man." He'd known Yakov since their earliest days in the army. They were in the same brigade their first year. As with any military group, those ties bind, especially in Israel.

"What's up? Any chance you're in Haifa? Is that why you're calling?"

"No, no. I'm in Tel Aviv," Noam said, pacing determinedly but aimlessly around his living room. "But I've got kind of a...funny question to ask you."

"Shoot."

"Do you know anything about Christian Holy Land Journeys?"

"Yeah, it's a company for Christian tourists."

Noam stopped pacing, bit his lower lip and looked to the ceiling. "Right," he said, his heart racing. "Exactly. I, um...do you know anything about their itinerary?"

After the army, Yakov became a career tour guide, a surprisingly high-level job in Israel. Guides must take a two-year course, spend nearly three months visiting and studying tourist sites, and pass written and oral exams from the Tourism Ministry before being allowed to show a single visitor around the country.

"I do. I've got a buddy who works for them. In fact, he just finished with a group a week or so ago. What do you need to know?"

"Well, uh. This is weird. I can explain another time but if someone began a tour a few days ago in Tel Aviv, do you know where they might be now?"

"I can find out. Let me text my friend. Hang on."

Noam resumed pacing, partly excitedly and partly disbelieving. Telling his mother about Chelsea was one thing. Getting a friend – and a friend of a friend – involved, that was downright nuts.

"My brother," Yakov returned to the line. Noam halted in front of the still-life strewn coffee table.

"Yes," he squeaked. If Yakov couldn't report where Chelsea's tour was, that was it. He'd never see her again.

"They're probably in Jerusalem or on their way there from Masada or the Dead Sea."

Noam dropped his head and exhaled silently. "Do you know wh–"

"One step ahead of you, brother. These groups stay at one of two hotels: Jerusalem Kings Hotel or David's Arches Hotel."

"Thank you."

"Hey, Noam. There's a girl involved, no?" Noam could actually hear Yakov smiling. But before he could answer, Yakov continued, "A Christian girl, obviously."

"I..." He didn't know how to respond. To some, a Jewish Israeli dating a Christian was an affront to the legacies of all who laid down their lives for the Jewish state of Israel. But to others, it was nothing.

"Hey, brother," Yakov said lightheartedly. "I'm cool. And that's what Yom Kippur is for."

Noam thanked his friend, grabbed his keys, a few changes of clothes and a sketchbook, and headed out to find a woman he hardly knew in the most complicated city on earth.

>>>>>>>>>>>>>>>>>>>>>>>>>>

NOAM HAD DRIVEN THE ONE-HOUR TRIP FROM TEL AVIV TO Jerusalem countless times. It was a drive not unlike those he'd made between Austin and San Antonio growing up when he visited his mother's family. Long stretches of highway, undisturbed flatlands interrupted by small swells of road too small to be characterized as hills. Occasional roadside stores and restaurants for travelers in search of gas, late-night pancakes or soda. In Israel, Noam preferred the drive back from Jerusalem to Tel Aviv. He enjoyed Jerusalem's windy, picturesque streets, observing the rituals of deeply faithful people of starkly different backgrounds, spotting the golden reflection of the Dome of the Rock from anywhere in the city, but he preferred Tel Aviv. To him, its soul felt younger, more current, more cosmopolitan.

The last time he'd been in Jerusalem was six months ago, to see Adi's family on her yarzheit, the anniversary of her death. He went every year. Once in awhile he stayed overnight and combined the yarzheit with a visit with college friends who lived in a nearby settlement. But this year, he wasn't up to it. He'd been tired – the sleeping issues had been as bad as they'd ever been – and he knew that the gnawing questions of faith would stir and bubble and boil over the longer he stayed in Jerusalem. So this year it had been a day trip.

To be sure, he was still tired. He wasn't sleeping for all the old reasons and for a new one too: Chelsea. And his uncertainty about God and belief continued to creep from the back to the front burner of his mind. Strangely, Chelsea was part of that too – not in a bad way but in a good one. What could he learn from her? Something, he knew it.

He plodded through the traffic that was a fixture of the westward trek into the city. It was barely mid-morning but the sun barreled onto the road. Droplets of moisture accumulated on the sides of his face. He pointed his nose down and sniffed his left underarm, cursing himself for not taking the time to freshen up before leaving. But he felt propelled. It was an unexplainable urgency – perhaps even laughable. But he needed to see this woman again.

Both possible hotels that Yakov had named were on streets Noam knew. He found the first hotel quickly. He pulled up to the front and told the valet he'd forgotten something at the front desk and would only be a moment. Noam felt bad lying but he couldn't risk missing Chelsea because he'd been circling around for a parking spot. He dashed in through the front doors, grateful for the blast of air conditioning the moment he stepped inside. It was a small hotel but there were dozens of people milling about – on the way to the dining room for breakfast, congregating in small groups on couches in the lounge area, and in line to check in. He stopped short, planted his feet and scanned the room like a basketball player surveying his next move. To his left, a uniformed bus driver held a sign that said,

"Jesus's Jerusalem Journey." Four women wearing hijab clustered to his right. The smell of buttery eggs wafted from the hotel restaurant.

He approached the front desk, past the people waiting in line.

"Excuse me," he said to the woman behind the counter.

"Hey!" someone with an American accent said from the line.

"Shhh," said another voice. "I read about this. Israelis do this. They cut lines. Just let it go. He looks big."

"Yes?" the front desk woman said, unfazed by his charging to the front. She was Israeli, Noam could tell, and he was grateful.

"I'm sorry. Very quick question. Can you tell me, do you have a tour staying here or about to stay here: Christian Holy Land Journeys?"

"I'm not supposed to give out that kind of information," she began, pausing to look Noam in the eye. She smiled shyly and added, "But let me see...."

He patted the counter as she typed on a keyboard. "Thank you."

"We've got several tours here today and tomorrow but none by that name," she said, blinking gently and smiling again at Noam. "If you'd like —"

"No – thank you. Got it." He nodded kindly to the people he'd cut in line and then jogged to the front door. "Thank you again," he called again with a wave to the woman behind the counter.

Outside, he patted the pocket of his jeans dramatically to the valet. The pocket was empty but he said, "Found it – thank you again!"

He hopped in his car and screeched out of the driveway on his way to the second hotel. He wouldn't let himself consider the possibility that Yakov's friend might not really know which hotels the tour group used, that maybe he wouldn't find her.

The other hotel was about a mile away and he inched toward it in traffic, tapping his thumb against the steering wheel at a speed he wished his car was moving. As he drove, he took in the city's stone walls, the cypress and eucalyptus trees lining the roads, and distracted himself from the absurdity of what he was doing by imaging which paint colors he'd combine to create precisely the shades of yellow and green that surrounded him. Finally, he spotted not only the hotel but a parking space across the street.

Was this a sign, he wondered? He knew how ridiculous that sounded. He didn't believe in signs. He believed in people. Someone who'd been parked in that space had recently moved. That was all. Still, Noam couldn't help but wonder if divine forces were at work somehow. He rolled his eyes at himself as he got out of the car and darted across the street.

This hotel looked much like the first, with the mid-morning rush of tourists eating, checking in, seeking recommendations, unfolding maps, gathering in groups. Methodically, he walked through the lobby, prepared to cut the front desk line again if he didn't see her immediately. A quick pass revealed nothing and Noam's shoulders began to droop.

But then he saw a new pack of guests exiting the dining room. Behind the group was a solitary figure walking slowly. It was the hair that he spotted first, that not-quite-golden, not-quite-brown head of straight hair. It was hair so unlike what he was used to – Adi's hair had been blond and thick. His mother's and sister's hair was dark and curly. This was shiny, wispy and thin. It was, unquestionably, Chelsea's hair.

Chapter Thirteen

"Hello, Chelsea. I really, really...don't know why I'm here."

She knew the voice – that husky tone, the Israeli spin on English, with its especially strong T's and D's. She didn't need to look up at the speaker to know it was Noam. Noam, here, in the lobby of her Jerusalem hotel. But of course she wanted to look up, to see him. In that moment, she realized that was precisely what she'd been wanting for days – to see Noam again. Looking at him now, at his dark, unshaven face, at the biceps pushing against his sleeves, at his insecure, almost impish half-smile, she felt a tremendous release in her body. It was like she could finally inhale deeply, down to her belly, for the first time in days, maybe even in weeks. She blinked back tears.

Thank you, Jesus, she thought. Thank you.

"You're crying...I'm sorry, I can –"

"No," she said, shaking her head and placing a hand on his chest. It was an instinctual move, but came with the side benefit of feeling his body underneath her palm. Her own boldness surprised her, though she didn't pull away. "No, I'm happy."

He placed his arm around her shoulder and they walked together to the nearby couches and sat down. As they turned to face each other, their knees touched. Around them, porters wheeled carts of luggage, kids ran by wearing swim goggles and carrying towels, three uniformed soldiers circled into the hotel through revolving doors. A bus screeched out air as its door closed and then rumbled as the engine started up.

Noam took Chelsea's hand. Before putting his arm around her moments before, they'd never touched like this. "Is this okay?"

She let out a small, confused laugh. "Is what okay?"

"This," he said, lifting their hands together. "And this," he added, looking around. "Me, being here. Me, holding your hand."

"It's fine," she replied, giving his hand a subtle squeeze. "But what *are* you doing here?"

He laughed. "You know, I have no idea. I really don't. I should be in Tel Aviv. I should be painting. I should be gearing up for a big work project I've got coming up. At the very least, I should be sleeping late this morning. But I wanted to see you again. I can't really explain it. I know you're just visiting my country. But the thought of you being here and me not being with you, not seeing you again. I don't know – it was like this uncontrollable thing. I had to see you again, even if just for a moment. I just can't explain it."

"I thought you don't believe in things you can't explain," she responded with a wink.

"I don't know what to believe anymore." He sighed and turned towards the chaos of the lobby and then back at her. "So is it okay I'm here? I know you have your tour...."

"Did you hear that bus a moment ago?"

"It's grainy but I really can't hear anything other than the sound of your voice."

"Grainy?"

"Grainy – you know, cutesy, schmaltzy?"

She laughed. "Ah, corny! Not grainy but corny."

"Now I'm doubly embarrassed."

"Don't be. It *is* corny – but I'll take the compliment. That bus was my tour leaving for the day."

He spun his head towards the front door. "Oh no, I–"

She placed her palm back on his chest. It wasn't necessary to make her point, but she did it anyway. "It's okay. They're sort of used to me ditching."

For a moment, they were quiet. Disbelief and excitement churned inside her belly. She could practically see her old life in Colorado – the life she'd grown up with, the life she'd planned for – slip farther away. A man in a suit approached Noam and spoke in Hebrew. "Ken, ken," Noam responded and slid closer to Chelsea as the man squeezed next to them on the couch.

She looked into his blue eyes. "What are we doing?"

"I have no idea. It's nutty – that's something my mom would say, 'nutty' – but I just want to spend more time with you while you're here. I know we hardly know each other. But when you left Tel Aviv, it was like I missed you, which was weird because a week ago, I didn't even know you."

She nodded. "My mom would say, 'It's bananas.' But I get it. I couldn't concentrate on my tour because I was thinking about the time we spent together."

Noam smiled his huge, wide smile. "So now what? I know you're here because you want to see the origins of Christianity for yourself. I can show you some of that. But, if you want, I can show you other parts of the Holy Land, *our* Holy Land, the one shared by Christians and Jews."

She shook her head, amazed at this place in life she'd landed. "I just ditched the international tour on which I blew my entire savings. My life at home is unrecognizable. I've become captivated by a man – a Jewish man, no less – I hardly know. This is crazier than a dog in a hubcap factory." She squeezed his hand again, a simple gesture that, amidst the bustle of a hotel lobby, felt intimate. When was the last time Austin held her hand like this? she wondered. Probably years. "In other words: why the heck not?"

>>>>>>>>>>>>>>>>>>>>>>

"THE OLD CITY OF JERUSALEM IS DIVIDED INTO QUARTERS," Noam explained after they parked his car and dashed across a four-lane street just as the light was turning red. "Jewish, Christian, Muslim and Armenian. There are seven gates into the Old City. This is the Jaffa Gate."

Dark-skinned old men stood outside the gate hawking postcards. Just inside, a barefoot teenager strummed a small, odd-shaped guitar with a high-pitched, tinny sound. It was still morning, but sweat dripped from Chelsea's temples. She imagined her eyeliner would smear and her hair would soon stick flat against her skull. On Christian Holy Land Journeys, she hadn't cared what she looked like. But now, with Noam, she did.

"Let's grab something cold before we begin," he said, reading her mind. They approached an outdoor stand where a man with a turban – a turban, in this heat! – was pressing fresh pomegranate juice. Noam ordered.

"I can't believe we're ordering trendy juice in the language of the Ten Commandments," she said.

"Hebrew is the only dead language that's been revived and then spoken by an entire country."

The turbaned man poured two plastic cups full of thin, blood-red juice and handed one to Chelsea with a smile. She was about to take a sip.

"Wait!" Noam said, grabbing a sugar shaker on the counter. He poured what looked like a half-cup of sugar into her cup. "You're good now."

The juice was perfect – tart, sweet, refreshing and most important, cold.

"You sure know your way around here," she said.

"I've spent a lot of time in Jerusalem. Every Israeli has."

"Why was that man wearing a turban? Is he Indian?"

"He might be. People don't realize how diverse Israel really is. Yes, we're a Jewish state. But people of all religions and backgrounds live here. Africans, Asians, Latin Americans, Europeans."

"I had no idea."

"Most Americans don't. That's why I'm going to show you my Israel," he said, flashing his disarming smile.

As they began walking, she looked away from him, ostensibly at the scenery of the Old City but in reality seeing nothing. Instead, her vision blurred as she wondered what she had done. What would he show her here in this ancient, foreign place? She'd come here to see how Christ had lived and died, to be reminded of God's goodness, despite what she'd witnessed back home. As good as she felt, she couldn't help but wonder if she let Noam's smile take her too far off that path.

"Here we are," he said, at once allaying her fears. "The Church of the Holy Sepulchre."

"Where Jesus was crucified and buried."

"Yes," he said, leading her towards it with his palm on the small of her back. They stopped just outside and he pointed up, to the church's facade.

"See that ladder?"

She shaded her eyes from the sunlight with her hand and spotted a nondescript ladder outside a window. "The wooden one?"

"Yep. That ladder has been there since the eighteenth century when masonry work was being done on the church's facade. It's called the 'immovable ladder' because no Christian order can alter any property on the church without consent of all five other orders. So...it stays."

She loved the way he spoke, the cadence of his words, the way his accent made her hear English in a new way. "Nuts."

"Yes," he said, leading her towards the church entrance. "It's not just Jews and Arabs who are stuck in nonsensical stalemates."

Just inside the door, they stopped again. It was dark and it took a moment for Chelsea's eyes to adjust. It was cooler inside, but not by much given that hundreds of people milled about, praying, taking photos, some even crying. To the left of the entrance a small group of men sat on a bench speaking what sounded like Arabic.

"See that guy in the middle?" Noam said. "He's the keeper of the key to this church."

"He's Muslim?"

"Yes. His family has guarded the key for centuries."

They walked through the different sections of the church, divided, not unlike Jerusalem itself, into various Christian sects. The building's age and decorative intricacy lent a spiritual power to the place itself. It was a sharp contrast, Chelsea noted with surprise, to Pulpit Springs, a place she loved but that she realized now was flat and emotionless with its mid-century architecture and uninspired grey and brown paint.

At the Stone of Anointing, where Jesus's body had been prepared for burial, Noam stepped back, giving Chelsea a private moment at what was to her, to any Christian, a sacred spot. She waited behind a dozen others – all women – for a chance to kneel before it. When it was her turn, she skimmed her palms along the stone, which was both smooth and rough, mostly shiny but also pocked with grooves and ruts. A shiver ran through her and a thousand thoughts and prayers raced through her mind.

"Thank you, Jesus, for bringing me to this moment," was the essence of what she felt. She whispered it and then added, "Thank you for your sacrifice for my sins."

As she stood, all that she'd been complicit in at home flashed before her. *My sins.*

"You okay?" Noam asked, placing an arm around her as she approached. "You look a little wobbly."

"I'm just hot. And this," she said, gesturing to the artifacts around her and then to Noam himself, "is all overwhelming. I'm so grateful to be here, to have arrived at this place, at this moment."

"You know, Jews have a prayer precisely for that feeling."

"Really?"

"It's called the shehecheyanu."

"The what?" She giggled.

"Sheh," he said, indicating that she should repeat each syllable, which she did. "Heck - eee - ah - new. It's the blessing of praise, a prayer to thank God for new experiences or just for bringing us to this moment. We say it on holidays. We say it the first time we eat a seasonal fruit. You might say it the first time a baby laughs or takes a step. Even the first time you kiss a new love." He gazed at her with his clear blue eyes.

"That's lovely," she managed to say.

They silently roamed around the rest of the church, past the Edicule and first-century tomb, then they exited the way they came in and turned left.

"You said, 'We,'" she said.

He knit his brows in question.

"A few minutes ago, you said, 'We say' that prayer. The shekilabu," she laughed, knowing she butchered the Hebrew. He halted, grabbed her hands and looked into her eyes, indicating they should speak together.

"Sheh-heck-eee-ah-new," they said, bouncing their hands up and down with each syllable.

"I thought you weren't religious. But you say prayers?"

They continued walking, weaving past Hasidic men and women dressed in black, through groups of Americans wearing athletic shorts and shoes, past packs of Europeans speaking languages as disparate as Dutch and Spanish. Stone pathways and buildings seemed to absorb and trap sunlight, brightening and heating their path. At one point, Chelsea spotted members of her own tour group heading towards them. She was tempted to bow her head and look away. But she had nothing to hide. She was an adult. And she was proud to be with Noam. When she realized that fact, she lifted the crown of her head millimeters higher towards the sun.

"You're right," he said. "I'm an atheist, at least that's the best word I can use to describe what I believe right now – or don't believe. But I did go to some religious school as a child so I know the basics, as do most Israelis. Though I'm not a fan of religious services, I do like some of the prayers, particularly when they are set to melodies, something that only happens in less observant synagogues. The orthodox do not sing, do not play music when they worship. But the reform – the less observant – do. My favorite religious services are actually those I've been to in the States, when my relatives had bar and bat mitzvahs in Texas. Their synagogue had a cantor – a clergy person – who played guitar and sang. She was like a seventies folk singer. I loved it. It wasn't spiritual to me but it was relaxing and...communal. So I know the shehecheyanu. But I don't say it on my own. When I have the first crisp apple of fall, I simply say, 'This is delicious – I'm so, so glad it's apple season again.'"

Chelsea nodded, silently enjoying his habit of repeating emphatic words. She felt differently about prayers and psalms and blessings. To her, they were magical. But she understood what he was saying. He had a way of doing that, of making her understand him even though they were so different. Her body flushed with this recognition. Somehow she understood

Noam. She was a devout follower of Christ – not just a believer but an active follower. And yet strangely, she understood Noam's perspective. She made a mental note to look up the English translation to the she-hecheyanu. What he had explained to her was beautiful and the prayer exquisitely captured what she'd felt inside the church at the stone where Christ had once laid.

Noam led her deeper into the Christian quarter and they paused at several Stations of the Cross along Via Dolorosa so she could take photos for Baylee. Once they'd roamed the full Christian quarter, Noam suggested they stop for lunch at a place he liked in the Muslim Quarter, a surprisingly short walk from where they were. Crowded and overflowing with vendors, the Muslim Quarter was comprised of stalls selling everything from pistachios, dates and spices to faux silk slippers and Harvard tee shirts. Old men sat in tiny corner cafes smoking hookah pipes. Holding her hand, Noam guided her expertly through the crowded shuk and eventually they turned onto a quieter side alley. Through one window of a closed stall, Chelsea observed men rolling out prayer rugs.

"Here," Noam said, as they entered a tiny restaurant with metal tables and chairs and linoleum that curled up in spots along the floor.

He nodded to the man behind the counter who, with the tiniest jut of his chin, indicated where they should sit.

"You've been here?" Chelsea asked.

"Tons of times." He spoke in Hebrew to the waiter, gesturing with his hands. As he spoke, she noticed the thick dark hair along his arms down to the back of his hands. She'd never known anyone with so much dark hair. Bizarrely, it stirred something in her. Hand hair is a turn on now? She couldn't explain it but she couldn't deny it either. When Noam finished speaking, the waiter grunted and made his way toward the tiny kitchen.

"You speak Hebrew to them?"

"They're Muslim but they live in Jerusalem. They know Hebrew the way local Italian vendors at the Vatican know English."

"Do you feel...weird...here?" she whispered. "In the Muslim Quarter?"

"I told you before, back in Tel Aviv, I'm a Dove. Not all Arabs are terrorists."

"These guys are not especially friendly," she leaned forward, gesturing to the men behind the counter with her eyeballs.

"No, they're not. And they may very well have terrorists in their families. They could even be teaching their children to hate all Jews. I know that. But if I'm one of the Jews who shows them respect, shows humanity, it's a small step that I can take. Plus," he added, "the food here is delicious. I hope you're hungry."

"That kind of reminds me of something," she said. "It's a dumb analogy to apply to the Israel-Palestinian conflict but here goes. When I was in college, I was in a sorority. Do you know sororities?"

Noam nodded. "Most Israelis probably don't. But, as I've told you three hundred times," he said with a wink, "my mom is from Texas. She went to UT."

"Right, right," she said. "Anyway, the older girls used to say, 'Be nice to everyone on campus because you may be the first or only Tri Delt somebody meets.' Like we were ambassadors or something."

"Exactly. For that reason, I feel almost a duty to interact with Arabs whenever I can."

"Well, I, for one, can attest that you're a terrific ambassador."

Her comment instantly embarrassed her. It felt effusive, even though it was true. Luckily, before he could respond, their food arrived, carried by a black-haired teenaged boy in a short-sleeved button-down and open-toed sandals. Noam had ordered several dishes, including lamb, lentils and no fewer than six spreads to slather on lavash bread. She hadn't realized how hungry the morning had made her. They ate heartily and mostly in silence, which felt comfortable rather than awkward. As she tore her second piece of lavash in half, her phone rang. She brought her brows together and darted her eyes sideways – anyone who knew her well enough to call her cell would also know that she was traveling in the Middle East. And for anyone who would call her from the US, it would be the middle of the night.

"Sorry," she said, pulling the phone from her small travel backpack. "Let me just –"

When she read the name on the screen, she sucked in her breath. Austin. With a trembling hand, she pressed the off button and quickly shoved the phone to her backpack.

Chapter Fourteen

"Are you alright? You look like you've seen a phantom."

Chelsea's complexion was pale, unlike how it had been moments before when they'd sat down in the restaurant after their trek through two quarters of the Old City.

"Like what?" she asked, shoving her phone deep into her backpack.

"Isn't that the expression?" Noam asked. "I've heard my mom say it. Like when someone seems inexplicably...terrified."

"Oh!" she said in recognition. She seemed to be forcing a light-heartedness that had been natural before her phone rang. She closed her eyes, took a deliberate slow breath and then smiled. "I get it. You look like you've seen a *ghost*. Not a phantom, but a ghost."

"They're the same thing, no?"

"Right. But the expression is 'You look like you've seen a ghost.'"

The grumpy waiter wordlessly brought another dish, chicken tawook. Chelsea seemed grateful for the distraction but Noam pressed. "So why did you look that way – like you'd seen a ghost? I don't mean to be direct but I am Israeli, after all. Who called you?"

She put down her fork. "My former fiancé."

"You were engaged?" Noam felt struck by this news, even though he knew he had no right to be. Of course, Chelsea had a life – had loves – before he met her less than a week ago. He himself had planned to marry Adi – before she was murdered. He wanted to tell Chelsea about Adi, about how when he met her she triggered emotions and desires he'd never experienced before. About the agony of her death, of hearing how they never found all ten of her fingers, how she was buried with only eight. But this was Chelsea's story now and he wanted to immerse himself in it.

"I was. His name is Austin. We'd been together for a few years, though I realize now the whole plot had been set in motion long before. My parents knew his parents, blah blah. We were engaged for nearly two years, living together for eighteen months."

"What happened?"

"He.... I...." She glanced at the napkin in her lap. "He disappointed me."

"So you cancelled your engagement?"

She nodded.

"When?"

"Three and a half weeks ago."

Noam choked down a bite of chicken and took a sip of tamarind juice to keep from coughing it up. "Three and a half *weeks* ago?"

She let out a whoop, a sound he'd not heard from her before. "I know. Bananas."

"This sparked your trip here? Your quest to reconnect to your faith?"

The cross around her neck bounced as she nodded. "I couldn't square Austin's behavior with what he professed to believe. I felt outrage, partially for me and partially on behalf of Jesus."

What had this man done? Noam wondered. "He's not Jewish," he said matter-of-factly.

"Of course not," she said. "I told you I barely know any Jewish people. But why do you say it like that, with so much authority?"

"I bet you five thousand shekels that there is not a Jew in the entire United States with the name Austin."

She giggled and her shoulders began to drop from her ears. The Chelsea he knew before the phone rang returned.

"And I bet there's not a Christian in the entire US with the name Noam."

"Let's call it even," he said and held up his cup to clink against hers. "I'm sorry, but can I ask: when you saw his name on the phone, you didn't look annoyed or sad. You really, really looked...terrified."

"You Israelis really are not into chit chat, are you?"

Noam remained silent, proving her point.

"Okay, yeah," she said. "I've got to get a handle on that. It's part of the reason I'm here, to be closer to Jesus, to feel safer with him."

"For a woman of faith, you sometimes seem as confused and scared as I do. Me, a nonbeliever."

She flinched slightly.

"What?" he asked, noting her reaction with a jut of his chin.

"'Nonbeliever.' I feel badly for nonbelievers. Not only nonbelievers in Jesus but to not believe in anything? It makes me sad."

Noam felt scolded, as if he'd disappointed her.

"But with you," she continued, "I especially respond that way because I don't actually think you're a nonbeliever."

"Even secular Jews have Jewish feelings," he said. "But you're changing the topic."

Her large eyes pierced him, and he felt she was steeling herself for what she was about to say.

"Without getting into too many details – *yet*, anyway – I looked terrified because I am terrified."

"Of Austin? Did he hurt you?" Noam sat up rigidly in his chair, preparing to unleash his IDF training on an enemy who was nowhere in sight.

"No, no he didn't." She grabbed hold of his hand, partly, it seemed, to calm him and partly to calm herself. "I'm terrified about what I've done to my life, of what life will be like when I go home."

"Go on."

"I'm a security junkie," she said. "My deepest, basest need is to feel secure. To feel safe. For life to be predictable, expected. It sounds boring but I've always been that way. In high school, we had to take one of those personality tests that gauged our interests, to help with choosing a college, choosing a major. Anyway, when I went in for my results, the school counselor reported that she'd never seen anyone with a lower score on the 'capacity for risk' section."

Then what was she doing here in Israel? Noam thought. Life here was always unpredictable with its rotating cast of characters trying to wipe out the Jewish state.

"I know I sound sheltered, even pathetic," she said. "But it's like in my genes. It's why I grew up loving church. The teachings and the community...the adults' certainty about beliefs...made me feel secure. When it came time for college, I applied to Colorado Christian College, less than two hours from where I grew up. I knew I'd be admitted and it was where several of my high school and church friends were going. It's where my parents and even my grandparents had gone. But a few months before applications were due, I heard about a small liberal arts college just outside Chicago. I don't know why but something about the school attracted me. It has this unique create-your-own major program. I thought I could take all kinds of classes – sociology, economics and," she held out a hand like an offering to Noam, "art history. Anyway, secretly, I applied. I even used my own money for the fee, and I was accepted, even with a partial scholarship. But I never told anyone. When it came down to it, the thought of being far from home, of living outside my comfort zone, going to a big city where I knew no one. In the end, I just couldn't do it."

Noam motioned to the waiter for the check.

"So," she continued, "my life with Austin was similarly plotted. I knew how it would play out – where we'd live, where we'd worship, what school my children would attend. Just how I like it. And it was playing out precisely how I'd expected. Until he did what he did."

"Then you ended the relationship."

She nodded grimly. "The only thing more important to me than security is my relationship with God. And staying with Austin, who claimed – loudly – to be a Christian, felt disloyal to God."

"And now?"

"And now my life is anything but secure and predictable. I read somewhere that divorce is like putting everything you hold dear on a picnic blanket and then tossing it all up in the air, not knowing where what you love will land. I didn't get divorced but that's exactly what it feels like."

"Explain."

"Because I broke it off with Austin, I no longer have a home since I was living in his condo. I don't know if I can return to my church, the church my family attends, the church where I grew up because many people will 'choose' Austin in this breakup – my own father has already done that. And taking this long trip, I'm not sure my job will be there when I return. And even if it is, I can't afford to live off my salary as a marketing coordinator at a hospital. It didn't matter before, because Austin has a good job. But now I must support myself, which of course any capable woman of my age should be able to do. But I never planned for this situation – emotionally or financially. I don't have a place to live. I don't even have a *toaster*."

The waiter arrived with the check. Noam paid, leaving a twenty-five percent tip, which he always did in Arab restaurants. "Would you like to walk?" he asked.

She nodded and they stood. She was farther from the door than he was but he came around to her side of the table and put his arm around her. "Please, continue," he said.

They exited the restaurant and turned onto the narrow side alley. He kept a protective arm around her shoulder. "I know I sound like a wimp, probably especially to you. Here, you live with bomb shelters and gas masks. Mandatory army service."

"Stop," he said. "Tell me more."

She took a long, weary breath. "For now, let me end with this. I looked terrified when Austin called because it reminded me of how little I have left. Of how I, a person who deeply values security and predictability, just disrupted not just my life but my future. It's like I'm homesick for something that no longer exists."

They meandered through the Muslim Quarter, its chaos and colors assaulting and soothing them. Being neither Christian nor Jewish, it felt, somehow, like neutral territory. Chelsea paused at practically every stall. At one displaying mounds of dried fruit, nuts and spices, she grabbed her hair in one hand and leaned way down to inhale the earthy, exotic scents.

A few minutes later, she said, "I could go for something sweet."

Noam took hold of her hand. "Come."

They twisted through more alleys, walked down shallow stairs, turned left and climbed up another set of wide stairs. Finally, they stopped before a teeny halva stall no larger than four square feet sandwiched between one stall selling electronics and another selling ancient coins. "My friend Yakov is a guide – he knows all the best places for everything.

You said you liked halva. According to Yakov, this is the best halva in all of Jerusalem."

Her eyes widened at the dozens of slabs of flavored halva, and he could practically see her mouth water.

"H'ky tov," he said to the shopkeeper, a young woman wearing a colorful scarf around her head. *The best.* That's how Chelsea made him feel – he wanted to give her the best. The best tour of his beloved country, the best food, the best of himself. The way she'd opened up to him made him want to do the same, to tell her more about Adi, about his art, his work. Even his somniphobia.

The halva woman cleaved a thin sample for her to taste. Chelsea shut her eyes, smiled and nodded. Noam ordered two slices for them, but Chelsea insisted on paying.

"Heaven," she said, holding with two hands the treat wrapped in wax paper. "I won't know how to describe this to people back home. It's so rich and sweet, but hearty too, almost like a meat."

"We'll get some more for you and you can smuggle it home in your suitcase." His heart burned at those words. He tried not to think about her returning to her home nearly seven thousand miles away. Everything about her – her delicate beauty, her faith in God, her openness to him and his life in Israel – moved him in a way he hadn't been moved since he'd fallen in love with Adi.

They spent the afternoon walking what felt like every street in the Old City. From the Muslim Quarter, they travelled southwest to the Armenian Quarter where she took photos of the intricate doors of St. Mark's Chapel and purchased a small ceramic bowl for her sister. Then they roamed through the Jewish Quarter, exploring the Judaica boutiques and tiny art galleries of The Cardo, the thoroughfare restored from the Byzantine era.

"Will you show me the Wailing Wall?" she asked.

"Of course," Noam said. "But no one calls it that here. It's the Western Wall or, better yet, the Kotel." He explained that the Wailing Wall was a pejorative term used by the British, who made fun of the emotion of Jews praying there.

A few minutes later, they approached what Jews consider the holiest place on earth. As the sun beat down on the tops of their heads, they emerged through metal detectors and then stopped at the place they were forced, as members of different genders, to separate. Noam walked into the men's side but paused short of the wall itself. He was not religious so unlike the hundreds of other men, many Hasidic like those Chelsea encountered on the bus the day they met, Noam would not pray at the Kotel. Instead, he turned to the right and watched as she walked into the women's side. She sat in one of the white plastic chairs, a few yards back from the wall itself. He watched her open her backpack, write something in a notebook, then tear out the paper and fold it up. She approached the wall, settling on a narrow spot between a squat older woman and a female soldier with a machine gun slung over her back. Noam loved the way she looked between them, with her denim skirt and Converse shoes. So feminine, so American. Like millions before her, she squeezed her note into a crack in the wall and then rested her forehead against the stone.

He wondered what her note said. He wondered whether her prayers might somehow include him. Were he a faithful man himself, he might have prayed that the feelings she gave him would somehow stay with him even after she returned to Colorado Springs.

Hours later, they walked through the streets of Jerusalem outside the Old City. They ate a satisfying dinner at a seafood restaurant and shared a bottle of wine from Fertal, his favorite winery in the Golan Heights. By the end of dinner, Chelsea finally lost the fragility he'd observed at the call from her ex-fiancé.

"I'm not ready for this day to end," she said as they strolled through Machane Yehuda Market. It was nearly nine-thirty but the air was still plump with heat.

"Then let's continue it."

They stopped at a small bar with an outdoor table for two. They ordered a final glass of wine, which they shared. Next to them, a table of thirty-something women laughed loudly together.

"The women here are just stunning," Chelsea remarked. "I mean, one is more gorgeous than the next. Look at that table over there – prime example. They're all so...exotic."

"You're beautiful too."

"I wasn't fishing."

"I know. Do you know why Israeli women are so pretty? Because they're natural."

Chelsea scrutinized the nearby table and nodded. "You're right. I don't think any one of those women is wearing a stitch of makeup."

"Same for you," he pointed at her. "You don't need all that goop on your eyes."

"Heeeyyyy," she said in mock hurt.

"I mean it. You want to look like an Israeli woman? Become more of yourself. Take away all that fake stuff. You don't need it."

She smiled, indicating that she understood his remarks to be a compliment. "Fair enough. I'll give it a try. Tomorrow, no makeup."

They finished the glass and continued through the Market, walking slowly on its slight uphill. That she'd implied she wanted to remain with him tomorrow sent a charge through Noam. It wasn't just the wine, it wasn't just that she was beautiful – and to *him*, exotic. He felt strangely linked to her, felt compelled to give her the security she craved. And she made him want to open up too, to share, to paint.

Finally, he couldn't hold back anymore. He grabbed her shoulders and pressed her into a doorway. He was gentle but it was a shove nonetheless. Yet she didn't appear frightened. Instead, she put her fingertips on his upper arms and looked up at him with those eyes, those beautifully shaped eyes with too much eyeliner. He wanted to capture their cappuccino color in a painting. He brought his nose to the tip of hers. She didn't pull away. He smelled the remnants of cinnamon hard candy on her lips. Without a word, he touched his lips to hers and felt the release of doing something he realized then that he'd been wanting to do for days. In reply, she squeezed his arms. With her lips, she responded.

"Yes," her lips said. "Yes."

Chapter Fifteen

Chelsea's ears rung as blood coursed through her skull. She was wobbly-kneed as they walked through the Market. She'd never been kissed like that before. Noam had taken complete control but remained gentle. So gentle. His lips were full and soft. His fingers stroked the side of her face and swept her hair behind her ear, sending shivers through her. He kissed her mostly with his lips but she tasted the inside of his mouth, which was warm and delicious.

They held hands as they made their way to her hotel. That they were headed there was unspoken, but as definitive as if they'd signed a prior agreement. She knew. He knew. As they crossed streets and weaved between groups coming out of restaurants and bars, she felt as if she were under water. Sounds were muted, everything appeared blurry. But she also felt calm, more relaxed than she'd been in months. Maybe years. She silently thanked Jesus for bringing her here, for introducing her to these feelings of attraction and tranquility that she'd never experienced before. She wanted to say the shehecheyanu.

Once inside her hotel room, Noam took her in his arms and kissed her again. More forcefully this time, but still with a gentleness that made her want to melt into him. He then brought his nose to hers. "I don't want to rush," he said. "Can I just...be here with you tonight?"

She was partly disappointed – for she could feel her body preparing itself for more – and partly grateful. His frankness jolted her back to reality. Here she was, in the Middle East, with a man she hardly knew. A man of a different faith – maybe no faith – a man with whom a future seemed utterly impossible. And yet she still felt in her bones that she was precisely where she was supposed to be, that it was God who had brought Noam to her. The situation felt, like many things in her life lately, out of her hands.

"I'd love that," she said. "I'm going to the bathroom. Be right back." She put her hands on his shoulders, lifted herself up on her toes and kissed his cheek, which had far more stubble than it had earlier in the day. Austin, she remembered, could go more than a week without shaving even once.

She used the bathroom, brushed her teeth, put rubbing alcohol on her new piercing and stood in front of the mirror. Her hair was tousled and flying away in spots. She wet her hands with cool water and smoothed it down, then leaned into the mirror. Did she look different? She felt different than she had a week ago, different than she had even this morning. Her skin appeared healthier. She took a damp cotton pad and removed her eyeliner. She was still no match for the spectacular Israeli women, she thought, pulling back from the mirror. But she did look more...something.

Before leaving the bathroom, she took out her phone and, without listening to it, deleted the voicemail Austin had left hours ago. Back in the room, she found Noam in a chair by the window looking through her stack of prayer cards, which she'd left out after reviewing some that morning. "I hope you don't mind," he said.

"Of course not."

"Do you read these every day?"

"Mostly."

"Why?"

"It grounds me, I guess. These are prayers and psalms I've heard my whole life. They're familiar. If I read some in the morning – or read a bible passage or something from a notebook I keep – it gives me a focus for the day. I've done it since college."

"I understand. Observant Jews are the same. Some – like my brother-in-law – start the morning with prayers and go to shul every single day."

"Shul?"

"Temple. Synagogue."

"Wow. Even I only go to church once a week."

"What would happen if you didn't read these cards or something bible-related?"

"Nothing would happen. I know Jesus still loves me, is looking out for me. I just might not feel as rooted in myself or in the world."

"That sounds like a nice feeling."

"It is." She sat down on his lap. "I usually read scripture before bed too."

"You're quite the reader, as I recall from our encounter at the cafe. And I see *Marjorie Morningstar* over there by the bed. My mom loves that book."

"My grandmother, she...had it sent to me." She moved from his lap to the second chair near the window and turned to face him. "Can I ask you something?"

"Of course," he said, gathering the cards and stacking them neatly on the little table.

"What grounds you?"

"Well," he replied, "not religion or spirituality. That makes me kind of...agitated because I don't understand it." He paused and looked towards the window, where the drapes prevented the harsh evening street lights from coming in. "Painting, I guess. Painting and sketching. When I spend time sketching the precise, irregular curve of an object or mixing the exact shade of a greenish grey that perfectly matches an object's shadow, that – I don't know – roots me, as you say."

She thought about his painting of the Begin Street signs that was nestled in the bottom of her suitcase. "That certainly comes through in your work."

They were quiet for a few moments, the electricity still there between them but at a lower voltage, like recessed lighting reduced by a dimmer switch. Mood lighting.

"Another question," she said. "Isn't it a fundamental belief of Judaism that God exists? That the Messiah will come? How can you be a Jew if you don't believe these things?"

"How can I not be?"

"That's what you said before, back in Tel Aviv. But I still don't understand."

"Many Americans, many Christians simply don't. And that's exactly part of it. Let's see...how do I put this?" He shifted, looked at the ceiling and rubbed his palms together. "I'm part of a tribe that's thousands of years old – and shrinking. I promised my bubbe," he gestured towards the copy of *Marjorie Morningstar* on her nightstand, "*my* grandmother, who wasn't even religious, that I'd never forget this magnificent group I come from. That I never forget the many groups, not just Nazis, who tried to eliminate us. From preschool, Israelis – even secular Israelis – are taught to never forget. It's why army training includes tremendous Jewish history."

Chills traveled up Chelsea's spine. Just then, her phone vibrated with a text alert. She pushed the off button without looking who had written. "Go on."

"What else do you want to know?"

"Well...if you're not sure you believe even the core tenets of Judaism, then what makes you Jewish?"

He laughed. "This is a good question, one I've thought about a lot. Being Jewish is a...wait," he pulled out his phone and showed that he was typing Hebrew into a translation app. "A *sensibility*. For me, being Jewish doesn't have to do with religion. It's a sensibility."

She rolled her hand to indicate he should continue.

"You're a Christian because you believe Jesus was the son of God who died for your sins. I'm a Jew because of my tribe – my nutty, hilarious, genius, *shrinking* tribe. My Jewishness is not related to the Torah, to attending shul. My parents, we joke that we are Jew-*ish*. It's that sensibility – our patterns, our judgments, how we, together, interpret the world."

"I sort of get it. Examples?" Though it was nearing midnight, she felt wide awake.

"Wait," he said, thumbing his phone again. "Here. Have you heard of Lenny Bruce?"

She shrugged. "Isn't he some kind of old-fashioned actor?"

"Comedian. A Jewish comedian. He did this whole bit about Jews and Goys – that's the Yiddish word for gentiles. It's really, really hilarious."

Noam hit a button on his phone and a grainy, black-and-white video played. Chelsea leaned in towards Noam, who smelled of wine and the sandy air outside. He rubbed her back as she watched Lenny Bruce explain that Jewish is pumpernickel, fruit salad and Ray Charles. And goyish is instant potatoes, Jell-O and baton twirling.

"Get it?" he asked.

"Not sure. It reminds me of this friend I had in college. She's black. She used to tease me about things that were white. Like, drinking to excess was 'so white,' she'd tell me. As were non-fat lattes and extreme sports. And 'going by' your middle name or by initials."

He laughed. "Exactly."

"It all felt kind of racist to me, but I think I see what you're saying. It is, in fact, a sensibility."

"Here are other examples: California is Jewish. Kentucky is goyish. But a black church in Kentucky is Jewish and a mega church in California is goyish. Hunting is goyish. Bloomingdale's? Jewish."

"I think I've got one!" she announced. "My father and Austin belong to Westberry, a men's club. It...let's see...the dining room tables are covered with fancy white table cloths but also have plastic ketchup bottles on top. Goyish?"

Noam roared and enveloped her in his arms. "Ha! You got it, you got it. Westberry: very goyish. Your friend from college? Regardless of her actual religion or background? Jewish."

Chelsea tried to kiss him but she was smiling too wide and he was still laughing. It made them both laugh more and then yawn. Gulping, loud yawns.

She brushed her hands along the top of his head. "Thank you for coming here, for finding me."

"I can't believe that was just this morning," he said, his eyelids closing. "I feel as if I've been with you for...well, for a long time."

"Me too."

"Can I sleep – *sleep* – here with you?"

"Of course."

They held hands as they moved onto the bed, still in their clothes. She rested her head on his shoulder. With her free hand, she stroked his face. He sighed and she felt all the muscles of his body release. Together, they slept.

》》》》》》》》》》》》》》》》》》》》

IT WAS THE HEAT THAT WOKE HER THE NEXT MORNING. THE
heat from the Middle Eastern sun warming the cloth drapes. Heat from
Noam's body next to hers. On top of the comforter, they'd slept back-to-
back, a position, she'd once read in a magazine, that signaled a couple's
solid, secure relationship. She lifted her head slightly and checked the
clock. Noam stirred at her movement, rolling over to sling his arm around
her waist. Friends would insist she should be wary now. After all, a man
she barely knew was waking up in her hotel room, a man from the other
side of the world. It was the stuff Carrie Underwood songs were made of.
But she wasn't nervous. In fact, she felt more content and more...herself...
than she'd felt in years.

"Boker tov," he said hoarsely. "Good morning."

"Good morning."

"And thank you."

"Thank you? For what?"

"Remember you told me about Austin – or at least part of what has
been troubling you?"

She turned towards him and squeezed his hands in hers just under
her chin.

"Well," he continued, "I, too, am not ready to tell everything but...
most of the time, I do not sleep."

"What do you mean?"

"I mean, of course, I sleep. But not like most people. I've got –
wait." He reached for his phone on the nightstand and typed a word into
his translate app. She heard a vacuum hum past the room in the hallway.
"I've got somniphobia."

"What's that?"

"It's a fear of sleeping. It's like...." He paused and she could see something akin to shame in his expression. She squeezed his hands tighter. "It's a clinical phobia. It's one reason I paint. I paint until I'm so exhausted I just collapse. I will tell you more, just as you may tell me more about Austin, some other time. But, for me, it's the falling asleep, that period between consciousness and unconsciousness, that involuntary dissolving, that surrendering.... Anyway, it terrifies me. Surrender is not in my constitution – I won't even use cruise control in my car. Lying in bed, when I feel that happening, I jolt up and force my brain to stay alert. It's unhealthy, even a bit unsafe. Last night, the way you touched my face and lay here with me, there was no in between. I just...fell asleep. So thank you."

"I've never heard of such a thing."

"I know. I'm weird. Most people love sleep."

"It's not weird. I'm sorry you deal with that. And thank you."

"For what?"

"For sharing."

Noam pulled her towards him. She reached around his broad shoulders and touched his nose with hers, the way he'd done the night before. And then he kissed her, another dreamy, slow kiss that began just with lips and ended with her wanting to devour every part of him – his mouth, his face, his whole body. It was then that she knew she was about to permanently alter her world and she was ready.

Wordlessly, they pulled off the clothes they'd been wearing since the night before. She wasn't used to intimacy in the morning. It was something Austin never liked. And for an instant she worried that her breath was foul. But Noam took her head in his large hands and brought her mouth to his, extinguishing that fear. He touched her everywhere, kissed her everywhere. She ran her hands over every inch of him, his thick body hair thrilling her in a way she'd never experienced. He was so different – so strong, so manly yet also tender. With the heat of the room and his touch, moisture quickly covered her body and she heard the rhythm of his panting match hers. He hovered over her, his blue eyes boring into hers.

"Is this okay?" he said.

She didn't respond but instead reached between his legs and placed him just inside her. A beautiful, animal sound escaped him. "Ohhh," he gasped. "Ohhhh."

As every muscle in her body tightened, twitched and then, finally, released, God's words rang in her ears: "'So they are no longer two, but one flesh.'"

Chapter Sixteen

"We're in trouble."

Chelsea looked up from the pages of *Marjorie Morningstar*. He'd fallen back to sleep – to sleep! – after they'd made love. And she'd picked up her novel, stroking his hair with his head in her lap.

"What do you mean?"

"We're like...connected now."

"That's one way to put it."

He sat up and brought his lips to hers, running his tongue over her one chipped and crooked tooth. He wanted to question her, to ask what was happening between them, to ask how they could ever be apart again. But he didn't want to break through the aura of mutual contentment in the room.

"You know, they call us Jews 'People of the Book,'" he said instead, gently removing *Marjorie Morningstar* from her hands.

She put her arms around his neck and he shuddered.

"So many times, I see you reading. Perhaps," he said, planting soft kisses on her cheeks while they both grinned, "you're actually Jewish."

They made love again, this time slowly. He wanted to extend everything – their exploration of each other, her pleasure. After a long, slow build, she cried out, a breathy, guttural cry. Climbing up from between her legs, Noam felt profoundly relaxed in his own body and uncommonly calm in his mind. Chelsea curled onto her side, the edges of her mouth revealing her satisfaction, and promptly fell back to sleep.

After a few minutes of watching her, Noam quietly rose and pulled a sketchbook and pen from his duffle bag. He sat on the chair by the window and began to sketch Chelsea's sleeping form. Figure drawing wasn't his forte but he welcomed the excuse to survey at length the curves of her hips, the way her hair – staticky from the friction between them – stuck in odd places to the side of her head and to the pillow. Normally, he sketched and painted to tire himself out. But as he cross-hatched shadows of her breasts, her chin, he felt more energized than he had in months, maybe longer.

>>>>>>>>>>>>>>>>>>>>>>>>>>>>

"I'M GLAD WE'RE GETTING A LATE START," CHELSEA SAID AS they sat side by side in a booth at the hotel restaurant. "So I don't have to explain to Kathleen that, yet again, I won't be joining the tour today."

"Who's Kathleen?"

"Our trip leader. I'm going to leave a message for her at the front desk and officially drop out of the tour." As soon as she said the words, a look of alarm crossed her face and she turned away. "I mean," she stammered, "maybe I'll catch up with them in a few days. I'm not sure what your plans–"

He play-punched her shoulder and then kissed her forehead. "Stop. Of course, I want to be with you here. Let's not focus on your home in

Colorado or mine in Tel Aviv. Let's not be guided by divine signs or the principles of science. Let's just be together."

She smiled as her shoulders withdrew from her ears. "Sounds like a plan."

"No plan," he corrected.

Wordlessly, they ate samplings from the breakfast buffet: sour yogurt and olives, toast and hummus and pickles. It had been an active morning and they were hungry.

"What are all these orthodox men and women doing here in this hotel? They don't look like they're tourists or guests."

Noam looked up from his plate and for the first time noticed the nearly ten male Hasidim, each sitting separately with a young woman. With only one exception, the couples appeared stiff. Then Noam looked behind their booth, seeing, as he expected, a much older Hasidic rabbi reading the newspaper in the corner.

"This is going to seem weird to you," he began. "But these are blind dates."

"At eleven in the morning?"

"Yes."

"In a hotel?"

"Yes. See that man behind us in the corner?"

She turned, craning her neck. He felt the sweetness of her breath on his cheek. "The one with the newspaper?"

"Yes. He's a rabbi and he's set all these couples up."

"Like an old-fashioned matchmaker?"

"Exactly."

"They don't know each other otherwise?"

"Probably not, no."

"So do they, do the women, get any say in the matter?"

"Perhaps. Depends on the rabbi."

"Oh my word," she said, choking on a sweet cracker called a kichel. "I thought my Christian church was conservative."

"Speaking of that," he said, tilting his head back as he finished his cardamom-spiced coffee. "I know you came to Israel with a purpose. I don't want to be the person who deprives you from that."

"So far, I don't feel deprived of anything," she said seductively.

He interlaced his hand with hers. "Fair enough. But we can spend time together while also fulfilling your goal here. I'm going to message my work and let them know I'll be using a few paid days off." He turned towards her. "So what would you like to do today?"

>>>>>>>>>>>>>>>>>>>>>>>>

NINETY MINUTES LATER THEY TURNED OFF ROAD 90 AND arrived at Qasr el Yahud at the Jordan River near Jericho in the West Bank.

"I can't believe I'm here," she said, as Noam parked the car. "This – right here – is where Jesus was baptized by John."

"It's also where the ancient Israelites crossed the Jordan River and entered the Promised Land after the Exodus in Egypt and where Elijah the Prophet ascended to heaven."

"You've been here before?"

"I told you," he said, taking her hand, "in the army, they take you everywhere and teach you everything. Soldiers must understand the sanctity of what they're protecting."

They approached the wooden stadium seating on the river's edge, the aroma of moss and moisture so thick they could almost see it. Everything was green – the lush foliage on the bank, the water itself. Dozens of tourists, barefoot and clad in white robes, waited in groups for their turn in the holy waters.

They sat a few rows back from the action. It was warm but overcast so the river had a pre-dawn, iridescent quality. Though there were dozens of people at the site, it was surprisingly quiet. Water gently splashed, small groups sang together as they waited their turn, the newly baptized cried in surprise and joy.

Chelsea's hand rested on his knee and he stroked its backside.

"Do you want to go in?" he said.

She shook her head. "I never planned on that. I've been baptized. I just wanted to spend time in the place of Jesus's baptism, the place that marked the end of his simple life in Nazareth and the beginning of his ministry. I wanted to feel close to Christ by being where he's been."

"Do you?"

"Feel closer to Jesus? I do." She rested her head on Noam's shoulder. "Thank you," she whispered, though he wasn't sure if she was talking to God or to him. It didn't matter.

A group of mostly black Americans were next. They wore bright white robes and clung to each other as they sloshed into the river. Several looked skyward and cried even before the first baptism. A young pastor gently took the hand of the first person in line, a middle-aged woman with close-cropped hair. He handed her a sheet of paper, encased in a resealable plastic bag to protect it from the water. She read, "Jesus, I commit this baptism day into your loving hands. By your crucifixion on the cross, I was freed from all sin. You were raised from the dead so that I, too, may live a victorious life, overcoming all evil. On this day, I rededicate myself to live a life for your glory." She handed the paper back to the pastor and plugged her nose with two fingers. The pastor took her head in his hand and she leaned backwards into the water. When she arose seconds later, an expression of delight swept over her. The others in line clapped. Some spoke out. "Praise God. Jesus is so good," they said.

Chelsea kept her head resting on Noam's shoulder as they watched the others take their turns. With each new baptism, the joy seemed to swell. The parishioners splashed in happiness and hugged each other. After the last person, they stayed in the water, standing in a circle holding hands. They sang what sounded like an old folk tune.

"Then sprinkle water on my brow," they sang soulfully, reminding Noam of the gospel choirs he loved, "as in this place I make my vow to own and love my savior now and give myself to Jesus."

"Are you crying?" Chelsea said, pulling back to look at him.

A ball in the back of Noam's throat prevented him from responding right away.

He nodded. "I believe I am," he choked with an embarrassed laugh, which made him cry harder. The poignancy of observing such a meaningful moment in these strangers' lives was nearly too much. He bowed his head and let the tears come.

She rubbed circles on his back.

"I am a Jew," he said emphatically. "I will always be a Jew. And I may also be an atheist." He felt her flinch ever so slightly. "Yet the joy, the intensity of what these people are experiencing.... This comfort, this certainty in God. I guess...I just want...something they have."

>>>>>>>>>>>>>>>>>>>>>>>>

THEY HIT TRAFFIC AT THE OUTSKIRTS OF JERUSALEM. AS THEY inched towards the city, Noam leaned his head out the window and glimpsed the hold-up ahead.

"Bomb."

Chelsea clutched the handle of the car door in panic. "What?"

Sirens blared behind and next to them, announcing the arrival of more police, who leapt out of squad cars. Taxi drivers with green and white Palestinian license plates got out of their cars and leaned against the doors as they smoked and spoke on cell phones. When the sirens faded, honking horns took their place.

"Don't worry."

"What are you talking about? There's a bomb?"

Just then, a muffled explosion pierced between their voices.

"Oh my stars!"

"It's okay," Noam said, scratching her behind the neck. It amazed him how her body felt like something he'd known forever. He could touch her anywhere, it seemed, and she welcomed it.

"What? How do you know?"

"Look," he said, and gestured to the traffic, which was quickly beginning to flow as normal.

"What exactly just happened?"

Noam leaned forward and pointed out the window as they drove past the commotion on the sidewalk. "It looks like there was an...unexplained? Unexplained?" he asked himself out loud. "Unexplained or...unaccompanied package. A package on the street with no owner."

"So?"

"So in Israel, that could be bad. They detonate unidentified packages."

"They what? Who?"

"The police. They blow up the package in a controlled setting."

"A controlled setting? On the sidewalk with all these people around?"

He shrugged. "That's what they do."

"And everyone was so...blasé."

"What does this mean: 'blasé'?"

"It means no one even blinked! Like, what if that had been a really big bomb? Everyone was so unconcerned. Just talking on their phones or whatever." She shook her head in disbelief.

"You're in Jerusalem, Chelsea, not Colorado Springs. This kind of thing happens every day."

He wanted to tell her more, about Adi and how she died, how instead of becoming more petrified of bombs after that, he was inured to them. He wanted to tell her about his unwillingness to surrender – to God, to terror, to sleep. But he sucked on one of the cinnamon hard candies she offered him and remained silent.

Twenty minutes later, they parked in the Ein Kerem neighborhood of West Jerusalem. After touring Marc Chagall's twelve stained glass windows at Hadassah University Medical Center, they bought coffees to go and began roaming through the streets.

"Why do you walk so fast?" he asked.

Chelsea paused and turned to Noam, who, she seemed to just realize, was nearly two steps behind her. "Was I?"

"You were and you do. It's an American thing."

"Really?"

"My relatives are the same way when they're here. And one of my friends at work grew up in Chicago. His legs are shorter than mine but I'm always behind him when we go to lunch."

"Huh," she said, reaching for his hand and mockingly yanking it as if to drag him through the streets.

"Yes, Americans are always in a rush. Here in Israel, we are mellower."

"I'm not sure I'd describe Israel as mellow. I mean, with your...sidewalk bombs...and soldiers with machine guns everywhere."

"Yes, but that may be why we have a relaxed attitude about everything. We know the value of living in the moment. We're acutely aware of our mortality but somehow that makes us fearless. We're not in a rush."

They continued walking arm and arm, taking in Ein Kerem's small alleyways.

"I can't believe we're still in Jerusalem. This neighborhood is like a pastoral village, not the city."

"Here we are," Noam said as they approached an outdoor structure with a large arch. The sun had emerged from behind the clouds that had covered them at the Jordan River and the structure's old stone seemed to sparkle.

"We're where?"

"Mary's Well."

Chelsea eyed Noam with surprise. She took out her phone and read out loud about where they stood. "'The village of Ein Kerem is believed to be the place where Elizabeth, the mother of John the Baptist, miraculously became pregnant and gave birth. During her pregnancy, Elizabeth was visited by Mary, who was pregnant with Jesus. The waters of this well are considered holy.'" She shook her head. "This wasn't on my original tour – I didn't even know about this place."

"I didn't either. But my friend Yakov, the tour guide, told me about some meaningful Christian sites you might like."

"Thank you."

She purchased an empty bottle at a tourist stand and collected some water to bring home to her mother. As they walked back to the car, Noam said, "I can't believe how lucky I was to be on that one bus on that one Shabbat afternoon."

"It wasn't luck," she said with the certainty of a physicist explaining String Theory. "It was God's hand."

》》》》》》》》》》》》》》》》》

THEY ATE DINNER AT A SMALL GREEK RESTAURANT NOAM
had read a review of in Haaretz. For him, the day with Chelsea had, once
again, felt like an instant and an eternity. She was so new and fresh and yet
also a soul he believed he'd known forever – or maybe it was more that he
felt she had known him.

"Can I ask you something?" he said. "You say that it was God that
brought us together on the bus, which was a wonderful thing – for me, at
least," he winked. "But what do you say when God lets you down. Like
what if we'd been on the bus and it got in a crash. Or if that bomb threat
earlier this afternoon had actually been real and we'd been caught right in
its crossfire. When something terrible happens, is that God's hand too?"

She put down her fork. "For an atheist, you have a lot of questions."

"That may actually be the hallmark of an atheist. I don't believe but
I wish I did. So I want to understand those who do."

She paused before answering. "This question is one I've asked
myself. It's partly what led me to this trip, to reconnect to God after it felt
like he let me down. With Austin and all...."

Noam nodded.

"Life is a mixture of happiness and despair, for sure. Bad things happen to good people. And the reverse is true. Even the most faithful people
have terrible things happen to them. I can see how that doesn't seem like
such a great system."

He laughed.

"I don't know the answers. I just have to trust that when things seem
like they're bad, that God actually knows what he's doing. One of my
favorite Christian thinkers put it this way: God is a package deal."

"I asked my sister Ronit this same question once. It was in two thousand eight when Hamas fired rockets into Israel from Gaza. At the time,

she was living in Ashkelon, not far from Gaza. I asked her if she was afraid. She insisted she wasn't because 'Hashem was watching over her.' Hashem is the Hebrew word for God."

"I understand what she meant."

"But I don't. If someone in her family had been hurt by Hamas, did that mean that Hashem didn't care about her? What then? She couldn't answer. And where was Hashem during the Holocaust? I don't get it."

"In these times, I remind myself something my mom always told me: 'Courage is not the absence of fear, it's the presence of faith.' She'd say, 'Chels, just keep your faith bigger than your fears.'"

He shook his head. "That sounds nice, but I still don't get it."

She thought more. "I know...I know in my bones that Jesus is good, that Jesus loves and is watching over me. But I won't say I haven't had crises of faith. Talking with you, it's helping me. It's reminding me, it's reinforcing for me what I believe."

The waiter took their salad plates and moments later another server brought lamb moussaka for them to share.

"For the last few years," Noam said, "I feel like I've just skimmed the surface of life. I want to believe there's something deeper out there. I see it in others – in my sister, in you. But I haven't found what it is for me. Maybe I never will."

"I bet you will."

"If I find something, it's unlikely to be the God you worship. It may not be God at all. I always joke that the closest I've come to transcendent moments have been in yoga classes. Maybe I'll become a yogi."

"I don't know. You seemed pretty moved by what we saw this morning at the river."

To Noam, that already felt like a lifetime ago. "Sure, I was moved by poignancy. But it wasn't spiritual."

"Well, be patient. Something else my mom told me: 'God remains close even when we are distant.'"

>>>>>>>>>>>>>>>>>>>>>>

BACK AT HER HOTEL, CHELSEA WENT INTO THE BATHROOM TO shower. Noam pulled out his sketchbook. Oddly, he didn't feel like drawing something realistic. Instead, he let the pen guide him, swooping and dotting in irregular shapes and patterns. It felt scary and freeing. After a few minutes, his phone rang. It was Yakov.

"How's it been going?" his friend asked.

"Great. She loved Mary's Well – thanks for the recommendations."

"What else have you been doing – besides the obvious?"

Noam told his friend about their tour through the Old City, the trip to the Jordan River. "It's weird. I really like this woman. Really like her. But she's...."

"American and Christian," his friend said.

"Right." Noam felt upside down, a nagging feeling interrupting his elation at finding what seemed to be the woman of his dreams.

"You're holding back, brother."

"A little. I mean, what is this exactly, what I'm doing? I'm not going to convert. She's not going to move to Israel. I'm not religious but I am a Jew. What am I doing with her?" He gestured around the hotel room even though his friend couldn't see.

"As a guide, I deal with a lot of Americans. And I must tell you, the Christians are some of my favorites."

"Really?"

"Really. They're the ones I keep in touch with the most. They get Israel. When tourism is down because of some Palestinian conflict or random acts of terrorism, the Christians remember me. They send me money unsolicited to sustain me during those slow times because they care about me, about Israel. It's why Christians tend to be Hawks."

Noam recalled political discussions he'd shared with Chelsea. She staunchly attributed the failure to obtain peace squarely on the Palestinians, citing the culture of violence against Jews taught in schools and broadcast in Palestinian media. "I had no idea."

"Most people don't."

"But think about it, Yakov. We don't wear Birkenstocks or drive Mercedes because they're German and we are Jewish Israelis who must never forget the Shoah. Isn't a relationship with a Christian akin to that? Aren't I, like, wearing Birkenstocks by being with her?"

"Noam," Yakov said, his tone both affectionate and scolding, "she's a person, not a shoe."

Chapter Seventeen

ust as Chelsea was checking out of the hotel, her phone rang. She'd been scurrying about the lobby, head down, hoping to slide out of the hotel – and her tour – undetected. She wasn't ashamed but she was confused. If she had to explain to someone what she was doing – skipping out on the tour she'd spent precious savings on to let a man she hardly knew show her around a Middle Eastern country – she wasn't sure she could do it.

"Mom, can you hold on a moment?" she said, sliding the room key and a note addressed to "Kathleen, Christian Holy Land Journeys" across the counter. She'd checked the group's agenda and set her alarm so she could awaken, eat and check out before the tour was even scheduled for breakfast. "Toda roba," she said to the woman behind the desk. *Thank you very much.*

"Are you speaking *Hebrew*?" her mother asked in an agitated tone before Chelsea had officially come back on the line.

"Mom, I'm in a Hebrew-speaking country. I'm saying thank you."

"I got a very alarming phone call several hours ago. From a woman named Kathleen. On your tour."

What? Chelsea thought. She doesn't even know I've officially abandoned the tour. Why was the woman calling the parent of a grown woman? "Oh?" she said in a neutral tone.

"Yes, she called us because we're on your 'emergency contacts' list. Let me tell you, Chelsea, that is not how I like a phone conversation from a stranger to begin."

"Sorry," she said, dipping her head and walking over to Noam, who was waiting on an oversized chair in the lounge area. She gave him a flat, no-teeth smile and indicated with her eyes that they could leave. He took her suitcase and grabbed her free hand with his as they walked a block to his car.

"This woman Kathleen said you haven't been going on the excursions. And she said several people in the group have spotted you around various tourist sites with a man, a man who is not on the tour."

"He's a friend, Mom."

"What is going on, Chels? I thought you were excited about this tour. All the money you spent...."

Something like resolve bubbled in her chest. "I was. I am," she said definitively. "A friend has been showing me around. I'm actually getting a more personal tour."

"I'm not sure I know what that means or that I want to know. You're running around with a stranger – and a Jew at that. I wish you'd gone on that mission trip with Baylee. Have you thought about what you will do when you return?"

"Mom, I'm a grown woman," her tone growing strong. "I'm learning a lot and healing too." She ignored the question about her job. The truth was, she was still afraid she wouldn't be able to support herself when she returned. Despite her strong voice, her shoulders trembled. That she might have to ask to live with her parents – and the specter of not even being welcome there – was too much to think about.

"Austin's swearing in is in a few days."

Chelsea swallowed and thought about Christopher Belford. Her resolve grew.

"Goodbye, Mom." She hung up.

She got into the passenger seat while Noam put their bags – her suitcase, his duffle – into the trunk. He got behind the wheel and looked at Chelsea.

"Everything okay?" he said.

"I feel like Marjorie Morningstar."

"Who?"

"The book that my grandmother sent me, the one your mom loves – *Marjorie Morningstar*. Yet again, my grandmother sent me a book that parallels my life."

"How?"

"Marjorie is young. She wants to be close to her parents and honor the way she grew up, but she also comes to think that she may want to live differently. She's trying to be, I don't know, authentic. She wants to be a famous actress with a glamorous stage name. Her parents want her to marry a Jewish doctor."

"How does she end up?"

"I'm only half-way through so I don't know yet." Can't she have something in between? Chelsea wondered. "To her parents, she's like a... commodity."

"That's how you feel?"

"Not exactly, though I do believe that once my father came to know Austin, I was some kind of...prize to lure him."

"So were you about to enter into an arranged marriage? Like the orthodox Jews we saw at the hotel yesterday?" Noam looked away from the road and eyed her with a twinkly expression.

"No," she said emphatically but then reconsidered. After a pause, she added, "But come to think of it, it felt that way sometimes. I've realized in the last few weeks that the pain of disappointing my family has been far greater than the pain of not being with Austin. So...maybe."

Noam squeezed her knee.

"Tell me, of all the books your grandmother has given you, which is your favorite?"

"*Anna Karenina*."

"Ah, Tolstoy."

"Have you read it?"

"No. But I've read about him and I believe he was what I am: a Humanist."

"Maybe you should read it."

"Tell me why."

"It's a long, sweeping saga, my favorite kind of book. And it explores themes of fidelity, passion and family."

"Sounds sexy."

"For that period, it probably was. But don't get too excited – it's also about social change and farming."

"Sounds a bit like Israel."

She looked out the window and considered that. "You're right."

They pulled up to Yad Vashem, Israel's Holocaust museum. She'd never seen so many tour buses – there were at least thirteen. As Noam turned the car off, she could feel his demeanor darken. "You ready?"

She nodded. "How many times have you been here?"

With an aura of sadness that she realized she should have predicted, Noam sighed. "Countless. And I will come countless more."

The outside of the museum was modern and tranquil, with sharp edges to the prism-shaped concrete building softened by sandy pathways and perfectly manicured trees. Inside, the museum was eerily quiet, the sound of feet shuffling through the museum's preset route the only indication of the hundreds of visitors. Chelsea led the way, exploring every single gallery shooting off from the main hall. Some of the video displays were too graphic to watch – children's skeletal bodies, newly dead, being tossed with metal shovels into huge troughs that adult Jews had been forced to dig. But she read every plaque, every quote on the walls.

"I do not know what a Jew is, we only know what human beings are" was prominently displayed in an exhibit detailing the work of Protestants to save Jews.

She listened to audio accounts, survivors with thick accents recalling with otherworldly dignity and calm the terror they'd experienced – their children being dragged from them at the entrance to concentration camps, their loved ones succumbing to disease on weeks-long train rides, being subject themselves to bizarre and painful Nazi experiments. At times, Chelsea felt dizzy and nauseous. Tears would not come but her body pulsed with perspiration even though air conditioning kept the building cool. She took off her Colorado Christian College sweatshirt and tied it around her waist.

In the vast circular repository of the Hall of Names, which displayed photos of thousands of victims (representing only a fraction of the six million), Chelsea realized that as revolted as she was by the horrors that were captured at Yad Vashem, she probably couldn't ever feel as deeply about it as Noam or any Jew. She felt her knees weaken. Noam seemed to sense it and laced his hand through hers.

Finally, after hours, they emerged to the outdoors, a glorious view of Jerusalem before them. Inside Yad Vashem had felt black and white and sepia. Now they'd returned to living in color.

"I feel as if I've been...underground for ages," she said.

"That's all by design," he explained. "Once again, despite senseless persecution, Jews survived," he said, pointing his nose to the vibrant metropolis in the world's only Jewish state. Homes, offices, highways, trees, ancient buildings, the Dome of the Rock all glistened before them.

They walked silently through the Garden of the Righteous, commemorating the gentiles who saved Jews during the Holocaust. The glimpse of humanity amidst the horror was the ending to their visit that Chelsea badly needed.

"Thank you for bringing me here. I am forever changed," she said, looking into Noam's eyes, which had a glazed quality she'd not seen before. "I feel weird saying this right now...."

"You're hungry."

"How'd you know?"

"It's a common phenomenon. Food helps us feel alive. It's human. It's not even lunchtime but you'll see the cafe will be packed. Let's go."

The scent of cafeteria grease assaulted them as they returned indoors. Noam was right – the place was crowded and the din had a nervous, frenetic quality.

"Yad Vashem brings out all sort of emotions in people – Jewish and gentile," he explained as they sat down with salads they'd made at a salad bar. "Relief, despair, guilt, faith, a feeling of Godlessness. All of it."

"I feel like I now have more of an understanding of the soul of Israel," she said. "And I have more clarity about what I learned last week at Independence Hall and the Palmach Museum."

"That's the idea. Israel takes its history museums really, really seriously."

The salad, featuring tasteless, limp vegetables, was the worst meal she'd eaten on her trip. She wasn't sure if it was the cafeteria setting or the intensity of the morning dulling her senses. As hungry as she was, she could only finish half the meal. She noticed the same of Noam.

"I'm not ready to leave," she said. "Can we go back to the garden?"

They found a bench outside. Noam took out his sketchbook. Chelsea felt as if rays of sun were shining directly on her like a warm, dry bath. She leaned back and closed her eyes. When she opened them again, she was astonished to see that more than a half hour had passed.

"I fell asleep," she said to Noam, who was typing a message on his phone.

"You did," he said. "I'm jealous."

She understood his meaning but didn't know what to say. He'd tell her more when he was ready, she knew. She picked up the sketchbook on the bench between them. He'd done three drawings – two of trees in the garden and one that was abstract and doodle-y but with an energy beyond the average doodle. All three sketches were looser, more abstract than what she'd seen in his apartment or in his paintings at the Nehama cafe. In the first tree drawing, he'd written words in quotes at the bottom: "'It seemed as impossible to conceive of Auschwitz with G-d as to conceive of Auschwitz without G-d.'"

"Who said that?"

"Elie Wiesel," Noam replied while continuing to type on his phone. "In his Nobel Peace Prize speech. Do you know him?"

"I've read *Night*. I'm a reader, remember?" she playfully nudged against him with her shoulder. "Why do you use a dash? You don't write out God."

"It's a Jewish thing. We're not supposed to erase or destroy God's name. And we should avoid writing it. Americans use a dash. In Hebrew, it's written in code. Many orthodox won't discard paper or books that contain God's name. Instead, they're stored in a genizah."

"A what?"

"A storage place. Or they can be buried in a Jewish cemetery."

"You follow this custom of not writing it out?"

He nodded.

"Even though you're not sure you believe in God?"

He paused and then grinned at her, the contradiction clearly just occurring to him for the first time. He looked down at the sketchbook in her hands and shrugged.

"I thought I'm supposed to be teaching you things here in Israel," he said with mock annoyance and then nudged her back with his shoulder.

Just then, his phone buzzed. He answered with a whisper. "Ken, ken," he said, "Check your messages. I just replied." After a few moments, he hung up. "Work," he said to Chelsea.

"All okay?"

"I've got a big deadline in a few days."

"I'm sorry. Do you need to–"

"Stop. Right now, I'm here with you." He kissed her cheek.

After a moment, sealing in what they'd experienced together at Yad Vashem, they stood.

Today was one of the most moving days she'd ever spent. She was with a man who made her feel things she'd never felt before – acceptance, keen interest. Though she felt as connected to him as a conjoined twin, a vast space still lay between them.

"This isn't real life," Chelsea said with a sadness that nearly overwhelmed her.

"No," Noam replied with a sigh. "It's not."

Chapter Eighteen

From behind the wheel, Noam glanced over at Chelsea, who dozed with her head rested on the passenger side window. It was remarkable to him how easily she fell asleep and how soundly she slept. Granted, Yad Vashem takes a lot out of anyone, the heavy emotion followed by the always manic cafeteria experience. And then they'd had that moment in the garden, the moment of shared recognition, of reality: they were strangers with wildly different backgrounds and wholly different lives in two very different countries.

Yet there was no denying that together they were radiant. Noam was both fascinated and calmed by her. But their time together was fragile. There seemed to be no way to permanently harness what was, perhaps, the best feeling Noam had ever had. That reality made him tired too, so tired that were he a different person, he'd pull the car over and rest the way Chelsea was. But sleep was something he feared and avoided. That hovering between consciousness and unconsciousness was to Noam like a drowning, a dissolution. That semi-sleep state felt chaotic and terrifying. The way the mind flitted unbound from song lyrics, to unexplained yellow hazes, to images of pets that had died decades ago, to lines from a work spreadsheet. Those in-between moments of not being in control of your own mind, of your body's impending vulnerability to the unknown terrified Noam.

In the army, he'd slept. Unending physical endurance tests, the relentless mental load of his responsibility to train diligent, capable soldiers meant that his body was too worn, his mind too bleary to experience even a moment's separation between consciousness and unconsciousness once he rested his head on a pillow. But after the army and especially since Adi was killed, he'd suffered. To Noam, sleeping was a surrender and he refused. Instead, he gripped and clung, jerked awake and gasped.

That Chelsea could sleep – so soundly that he could hear faint snores – alongside someone she barely knew in a country where she had no one to trust, was a deep compliment to Noam. It was also a testament to her faith – in him and in her God.

They were driving to Safed, a hilltop town in the upper Galilee about two hours north of Jerusalem known for its art galleries and links to Kabbalah. It wasn't on Christian Holy Land Journey's itinerary but it was one of Noam's favorite towns and he wanted to show Chelsea. He'd spent many long weekends in Safed, with his family, with his army and college friends, with Adi. He loved its twisty narrow roads, which could lead you anywhere: to a tucked away cafe with a view of the valley below, to a tiny, hundreds-year-old synagogue, to a flashy art gallery with surprising wooden sculptures. He knew just the place for them to stay, not in Safed itself but in Amuka, a mitzpe, a small communal village nearby.

Chelsea woke as he was circumventing the base of Safed and heading toward Rosh Pina.

"Good rest?"

She inhaled deeply and smiled. "Yes. I feel refreshed." She placed a hand on his leg, sending a charge through him.

"We're going to check into a tzimmer, drop off our bags, and then we can explore Safed."

"Tzimmer?"

"Ah, I believe you call them breakfast in beds?"

She looked confused but then lit up with recognition. "A bed and breakfast!"

"Ken, ken."

He turned onto a narrow, almost hidden road, and the scent of pine quickly filled the car.

"It smells like home," she said. For a moment, a dark pall crossed her face. But she was soon distracted by hoards of young men in black suits walking with purpose down the road.

"What's going on here?"

"Ah, I forgot what else is here."

They hit the mountain summit and saw signs, several handmade, pointing to a deep valley where the men where heading.

"Amuka is home to the grave of Yonatan Ben Uziel, a rabbi from the first century. He was a student of the famous Rabbi Hillel."

"Why are so many young men – Hasidim – going there?"

Noam slowed the car to let some of the boys pass and then made a sharp right. "I'll show you."

They drove deeper into the valley, following the young men's path. The unkempt road, with large pines giving way to oak and walnut trees, was quiet except for the boys' lively chatter.

Finally, they parked near a large, white rectangular structure.

"This is the tomb?"

Noam nodded.

"Why are all these excited young men, the ones with – what are those long curls on the side of their heads?"

"Payot."

"And what are they carrying?"

"Siddur. Prayer books."

"Why are they all here?"

"Rabbi Uziel never married and regretted that. Legend says that before he died, he promised that anyone looking for their beshert should pray at his grave and their prayers would be answered."

"What's a beshert?"

"It means...destiny. And in the case of love, it means your...intended."

She looked around and smiled.

"This place does feel sort of...magical."

Noam looked into her eyes, the color of the walnuts on the trees surrounding them. He wanted to envelop her, to be enveloped by her. "Many say it is. Let's go."

As they walked, she pointed to scarves, shawls and hats hanging from low tree branches, many with notes attached to them. There were also pieces of paper stuck into crevices of the tree, not unlike the Kotel. "What's all this?"

"Some people write messages to help find their beshert. They use clothes to tie them to the branches. And...those clothes also have names and phone numbers on the labels," he said in a knowing tone.

"Ahhhh," she said. "So one of these young men may call and say, 'I found your scarf.'"

"Exactly. Many couples have been formed this way, which, of course, begs the question. Was it the prayers at Amuka or a person simply taking charge of their life?"

She took his hand as they walked. "I believe the prayers were answered, even if they got a little head start."

"You're not alone. David Ben-Gurion, Israel's first Prime Minister, famously said that anyone who doesn't believe in miracles isn't a realist."

She laughed. "I've heard of many miracles in my short time here. The Six-Day War, when Egypt sent tens of thousands of troops to obliterate Israel, and Jordan and Syria attacked using Soviet weapons. Somehow teeny, tiny Israel managed to destroy hundreds of Egyptian planes, drive Syria from the Golan Heights and capture all of Jerusalem? That was nothing less than a God miracle - and just one of the many I've heard here."

"Maybe you should be both an Israeli and a realist."

She looked at him with an expression he couldn't identify.

"What?" he asked.

"I'm learning that sometimes you can be disagreeable."

"Now you're becoming like a blunt Israeli...."

"Perhaps. But can you be convinced of *anything*? Or do you just prefer a point-counterpoint discussion format?" Her question was pointed.

"Ah, you must not have heard the age-old joke: two Israelis, three opinions. We're Jewish. It's our culture to discuss, question and argue. It's what my orthodox brother-in-law does all day long – debates the meaning of Torah passages with other devout Jews. But even the secular among us like debate. It's like an Israeli national pastime. To us, it's not arguing, it's discussion."

She partly nodded, partly shrugged, apparently unsatisfied. They walked up to the tomb, which was surrounded by dozens of boisterous men. Some held siddur, some giggled with nervous laughter and punched each other playfully. Their youth, their enthusiasm filled the air as much as the nut trees tossing dark afternoon shadows on the tomb.

Noam marveled at how the boys seemed wholly *in* their lives, that they'd fully accepted where they'd landed by birth. Did they even know the extremity of their traditions? Did they know there were other ways to be Jewish? Did they know that at, say, a synagogue in San Francisco, they could sing their prayers and even sit alongside their wives, mothers and sisters? That they could pick a spouse of their own choosing, perhaps even someone of another religion or even gender?

"I know we drove downhill and that we're in some kind of valley," Chelsea said with the serenity he admired. "But I feel especially close to heaven right here."

He wanted to agree – because he, too, felt something transcendent with her there at an ancient rabbi's tomb amidst dozens of young orthodox men. But he didn't believe in heaven. The contrast between her words and what he felt blanketed him with disappointment. *How could he make himself believe?*

"The words of Genesis come to mind," she continued. "'Male and female, He created them.'"

Hands laced, they walked around the small tomb together, observing the visitors as much as the tomb itself. Among the orthodox men were a few teenage girls, whose demeanors were far more solemn than that of the boys. Though Noam had seen these orthodox teens his whole life, they suddenly struck him as so incredibly young.

"Do you believe in one true love?" she asked.

"I believe in true, deep, spellbinding love."

"Have you been in love like that?"

He turned to look her in the eye. "I have." And then he told her about Adi. About her thick blond hair, her embarrassingly loud laugh, her nerdy glasses, her fierce intelligence. Once he spoke of her, he couldn't stop. He told Chelsea about how excited he was to propose, about the horror of her death at the hands of a suicide bomber just days before he was able to. Three large tears dropped as he spoke. By the time he finished, she was crying too. He was grateful that she didn't say much in response to his story. She simply said, "I'm so sorry" and hugged him tight.

Wordlessly, they walked outside, circling the perimeter of the tomb, pausing beneath the trees strewn with notes and articles of clothing. Chelsea appeared mesmerized as she tried to glimpse words on the notes without disturbing them. Noam felt high on the fresh aroma of pine. Behind them, a new hoard of Hasidim clomped down the hill while the ones who had said their prayers to meet their beshert began the long walk up the hill.

He wanted to be like them both – the Hasidic boys and Chelsea – both so full of faith. He wanted to believe that problems, heartaches and wishes could be successfully addressed through prayer. But the longing itself revealed how truly removed he was from the observant Jews and the Christian woman for whom his heart was expanding.

Even if she didn't live seven thousand miles away, even if she lived right here, right beside him, would being with Chelsea mean being like her? The prospect of turning his life over to God felt at once like a profound relief and yet also utterly impossible.

A scientist rooted in proof, he did not believe in Creationism. He did not expect to meet God in Heaven. Virtually every "miracle" story he'd heard could be explained through science or history. Modern Israel existed not because God specially blessed the country but because of the Iron Dome, because of great minds.

They stood arm in arm beneath a tree and Noam placed his chin on the top of her head, inhaling the jasmine scent of her shampoo. Religion was not just a belief system for her. It constituted the very structure of her life – everything from morning devotions with prayer cards to lunches every single Sunday after services. Noam, on the other hand, was guided solely by what was in front of him – the data at work, the whims and desires of his family and friends, the objects he arranged for still lifes to paint.

Chapter Nineteen

"Will you tell me now?"

They were sitting in a small Arab restaurant, a hole in the wall just outside of Safed, where they'd spent the last several days roaming the cobblestone alleys and perusing little shops selling everything from cheese to candles. Among her favorite stops was the twenty quiet minutes they spent at the Abuhav Synagogue, which, Noam explained, was built by Sephardic Jews, those of Spanish or Portuguese descent. She took nearly fifty photos of the building's stunning light fixtures and carvings. The colorful oval dome featured paintings of biblical scenes she'd studied her whole life.

They'd also taken an afternoon to visit the Mount of Beatitudes, which was a place she'd been looking forward to visiting with her tour. The site, at Mount Eremos on the northwest side of the Sea of Galilee, is where Christian scholars believe Jesus gave his Sermon on the Mount, the first of five lessons setting forth his moral principles, what many believe were his commentaries on the Ten Commandments. She'd felt such peace there, with Noam's arms around her, knowing that Jesus had been in that very spot. Everything she'd experienced in Israel – the culture, the history,

the scenery, the people – was so rich. It was the only place, the only location she'd ever been that felt as if it had a soul.

"Tell you what?" She was scooping large spoonfuls of smoky baba
ganoush onto pita bread, washing every bite down with sugared mint tea.
She'd become so accustomed to the spices and textures of Israeli and
Arab food that she wondered how she could return to her normal diet
of oatmeal, turkey sandwiches and garden salads when she returned to
Colorado Springs.

"About Austin."

Chelsea flashed back to that moment when she first knew she had
to come to Israel. With Beth long gone from the hospital, she'd taken to
spending her lunch hours reading. The days following her break up, she
simply didn't have the energy or the focus to read a novel so she borrowed
a few magazines from the ER waiting room. She paged through Easter
dinner ideas (the hospital's magazines were always many months old) and
spring gardening tips with nervous energy, barely reading, barely eating.
But one day, a story in a news magazine caught her eye. It was a look back
on the life of Neil Armstrong. The astronaut had been quoted as saying that
visiting the Temple Mount in Jerusalem, a place where Jesus himself had
once walked, had been more thrilling to him than setting foot on the moon.

Chelsea had spent the previous days heartsick. Not only had she
broken her engagement, but her view of Christianity suddenly took on a
different texture. To her, it suddenly felt less about Jesus, and instead had
become about the faithful trying to shape society, about a lust for power,
about force and shame. Christ's original teachings – peace, compassion,
humility, love, charity – had somehow become lost. Not only did she feel
like an accomplice to what her father and Austin had done, but, strangely,
no one else – her mother, Baylee, Crystal – seemed outraged. What did
that say about the values of her Christian community?

In those days, Chelsea wrote in her journal, "Jesus does not waste
our pain" over and over, as if to convince herself. She prayed for answers.

The day after reading Armstrong's account of his Israel trip, *Eat Pray Love* arrived special delivery from her grandmother. Once again, God had answered her in unexpected ways. That night, she spent hours researching tours and by the next morning, she'd made a reservation, purchased a plane ticket and requested extended, unpaid leave from her job.

In the Arab cafe, she slowly chewed her pita bread and glanced up to the wall beside them, where black and white photos of presumably famous Arabs were hung. She hadn't thought about Austin in days and the mention of his name, conjuring everything she still had to face at home, added a bitterness to the food that moments ago had been so tasty. Yet she knew Noam deserved to hear the whole story, the story that led her to need to be closer to Jesus by traveling to the place he'd lived.

She took a breath. "So I told you that Austin and I dated for many years and that my parents loved him, especially my father."

"Ken." He'd taken to speaking the simplest words to her in Hebrew, which she loved. Ken. Toda. Yo-fee. *Beautiful*.

"So Austin was – is – a real estate broker by trade. But he had mild ambitions to go into politics. My father is a frustrated politician himself. He never ran for anything but I think he would if he could do it all over again. He's president of Westberry, the men's club in town. He's also a bit of a behind-the-scenes power broker in city politics. So when he learned of Austin's blooming interest in politics, he saw an opportunity. He doesn't have a son so –"

"What does *that* have to do with anything?"

She gestured, signaling that the sexism was apparent to her too. "I know. But to be fair, it was patently clear that neither Baylee nor I had an interest in carrying out his political ambitions."

He nodded, and she could tell he was trying to keep his expression neutral. "Continue."

"My dad is pro-development, anti-tax. About a year ago, he learned that a position on the city council would be opening up because an old guy, someone he knew from our church, was planning to retire. At that point, he began to groom Austin for the job, plotting his...wait for it...pro-development, anti-tax campaign. They worked together for months so when it came time to file papers to run, their whole campaign strategy was already in place."

"Yes," Noam said to indicate his understanding.

"Austin's opponent was a guy named Christopher Belford. Not only was he liberal – a position my father detested – but he is gay."

Noam raised his eyebrows as if to say, "Now we're getting somewhere."

"The campaign went the way you'd think, my father harnessing the power of living for decades in The Springs and knowing all the important players. Belford had the endorsement of a liberal college in the city, but Austin was the frontrunner. Looking back, I held my breath the whole time, hoping that Belford's sexual orientation wouldn't be a point of contention."

"Was he already out?"

"Yes, thankfully, he was. Neither my father nor Austin even knows any gay person. Not one. But that didn't stop them from despising homosexuals – *all* homosexuals. On the singular ground of their homosexuality. Me? The Christian thing is to like or not like someone based on their character – not on their characteristics." Memories of working alongside Beth – the laughs they shared, their long, deep conversations – flashed in her brain.

"That's the human thing to do," Noam said.

"Right. So I was relieved that Belford's sexual orientation was only referenced by Austin in subtle ways. During campaign events, he'd talk about his 'pro-family' platform. The official campaign photos included me. It was a 'look at this cute, young couple on the verge of beginning their lives together' kind of thing."

Noam sat back a little in his chair, and Chelsea could practically smell the sarcastic remark that rested on his tongue. She appreciated that he didn't actually say out loud whatever it was.

"Sooooo," she continued, "unsurprisingly, Austin won the election. My father threw a huge bash on election night in our church social hall. Austin held my hand throughout the entire event. I felt like, I don't know, a First Lady or something."

"So far, this sounds like standard American politics. Nothing to cancel an engagement over."

"Right," she said, pointing at Noam. "That's what I thought. But in the weeks after the election something else happened."

He leaned forward and took a sip of his tea.

"I guess my dad had done some due diligence on Belford. I don't know if that's standard procedure for city politics but there it was."

Noam waited with an impartial expression.

She gathered fortitude with an inhale. "Through this secret investigation, he learned that in the past, Belford had been...in an abusive relationship." Regret bubbled in Chelsea as she recalled those weeks. "Somehow my dad obtained police evidence photos of Belford with a black eye, and his ear and bottom lip newly stitched." Her voice caught as she spoke.

"He was the *victim* not the abuser?"

"Yes."

"What happened?"

"After the election – *after* Austin had won – they leaked the photos and the story of the abuse to the newspaper. It caused a bit of an uproar. I mean, some people felt badly for Belford. I certainly did. The man had been beaten, after all. But others wrote letters to newspaper editors and comments on social media about how lucky the city was not to have elected a...pussy...to public office."

"I'm sorry. I am not understanding. Why would your father and Austin do this? He'd won already."

Her throat constricted. "This is the part...I, I don't know."

"He wanted simply to humiliate an opponent he'd already beat?"

She forced herself to hold his gaze as she nodded her head.

"With nothing to gain...," he said. "That's...that's hateful."

The shame that launched Chelsea out of her life and into the Middle East hovered in her solar plexus. Without anything to gain, Austin and her own father had humiliated a man for the sole reason that his values were different from theirs. Their smear campaign of Belford, who'd already once been a victim of abuse, was cruel, premeditated and, worst of all, gratuitous.

"Did you discuss it with Austin? Your father?"

She shook her head. "I tried to. Whenever they were together, they just talked about the policies he'd promote once in office. When I was alone with Austin, he dismissed me. Told me to get over it, that it was part of politics. When I brought up how unchristian his behavior had been, he blamed my dad."

"Wow."

"There's more. A few weeks after Belford lost the election, his old boyfriend – the one who'd beaten him up – resurfaced. His identity had been leaked too and he lost his job as a result. He was furious and began harassing Belford – threatening him over the phone and smashing up his car."

Noam shook his head in disbelief.

"A week later," she choked, "Belford hanged himself."

She bit her lip to stop it from quivering. Memories of the post-election weeks, the congratulations she received at work, in the supermarket, at church, the shame she felt at Austin's and her father's inexplicable meanness, it brought bile to the back of her throat. "Everyone was congratulating me on Austin's win, and I felt unable to express my disgust over what they'd done. And then after Belford killed himself, I felt like some sort of...accomplice."

"I can see that," he said.

She felt the blood drain from her face, felt that shame all over again.

Noam reached for her. "But if you are a Christ follower, then you should know that you deserve mercy. In that pivotal moment, your values – good values – were revealed."

She hung her head and let the tears fall onto her plate. "There's something else," she said. In many ways, this was the worst of all.

He squeezed her hand. "It's okay."

She was crying harder now. "Once Austin and I got serious, and my family got serious about us, I felt like I was on a runaway train. Long before the election – long before our engagement – I had this odd feeling. It wasn't a realization because it never quite hit my consciousness. But it was something that was always there, lurking in my mind but surfacing only when I sat still. I don't think...oh God...I don't think I ever loved Austin."

Noam squeezed her hand again, giving her strength to continue her admissions.

"Everything seemed to be aligning. I'd met a man who checked boxes: smart, successful, likable, similar beliefs, similar life goals. It's what people were doing: pairing up, starting lives and families together. It was like musical chairs and I had found a seat right as the music was stopping. Even though I didn't feel passion for Austin, I loved the life that being with him promised. When he asked me to marry him, what was I going to say – no?" She shook her head in small, almost violent movements. "It would have been...unthinkable."

She moved a piece of hair behind her ear with her free hand, which was shaking. Noam grabbed hold of it, comforting her, warming her, accepting her.

"It felt like love, what I had with Austin. But looking back, it was really just companionship. He was a partner – in my family, in my future. It was transactional." She dropped her chin again and let the tears come. "I'm so ashamed. For getting on that runaway train, for staying quiet about what they did to Belford. And as unthinkable as it would have been to say no to Austin's proposal, I ended up doing something equally unthinkable: I tossed my manicured, carefully planned life up into the air."

"So that's why you wanted to come here?"

"I couldn't understand how my father, Austin, my community could be Christian when such an unholy act of meanness had been condoned. And my father was – is – furious with me for leaving Austin, for disrupting the picture-perfect image he'd helped create. After all of that, my beliefs were stripped down. I needed to square everything back up. For remaining silent about Belford, for going along with a relationship that never felt exactly right, maybe I came here looking for what you said, for mercy."

"And?" he asked.

"I may have found something even better. I found you."

)»»»»»»»»»»»»»»

THE NEXT EVENING, NOAM TURNED THE CAR OFF ROAD 90 and pointed to houses they passed on the way to Hukuk beach.

"Did you know that ninety percent of Israeli rooftops have solar power?"

"Impreeeeeeesssssssive," Chelsea replied with mock enthusiasm. The last few days she'd begun teasing him about his prideful command of facts about Israel.

"I know," he said, not yet catching her playful sarcasm. "We have three hundred days a year of sun here. It'd be criminal not to harness that energy."

She turned her body towards him and massaged her chin as if in deep thought. "Criminal, indeed."

He glanced over at her and then did a double-take, finally grasping her teasing tone.

"Funny," he said.

"No," she said, pinching his earlobe. "You're funny."

"Listen, the only way I can feel okay about snatching you from your tour is by giving you the best tour I know how."

"I'm just kidding around," she said, patting his thigh. "This definitely is the best tour. Tell me more."

He sat up straighter and assumed a deep, authoritative voice.

"The Israeli coast runs one hundred and seventy miles." He paused and winked at her. "But this particular beach we're going to is not on the coast. We're on the western side of the Kinneret, which you may know more commonly as the Sea of Galilee, though it's not actually a sea – it's a lake."

"Now that *is* interesting – or at least confusing."

"My favorite beach in all of Israel is Michmoret beach, but that's a few hours from here. When David texted about meeting up for a beach rave, I suggested Hukuk, since we're in the north."

"He didn't mind schlepping here from Tel Aviv?"

He pointed at her. "Excellent." He'd been teaching her common Yiddish phrases – meshugenah, mishpucha and, of course, shtup, phrases his American mother grew up using. "David is actually coming from Haifa, which is a little closer but, no, he didn't mind. No one here will mind. If they mind, they don't come."

"Logical."

"Fact: Israelis love beach parties. When I was in high school, I used to take the bus up to Michmoret and stay overnight under the stars with my friends."

"Your parents let you do that?"

Noam nodded. "Everyone's parents do. Rave parties on the beach are just part of the culture. It's like our...response...to our parents' and grandparents' generations. They were consumed by the Holocaust. So we are consumed by life."

Despite her teasing, the fact was that she truly did enjoy Noam's frequent fact-spewing, especially tonight. It took her mind off the fact that she was about to do something she never anticipated: meet some of Noam's friends. What would they think of her, a shiksa? Would they compare her to Adi? Would Noam behave differently with them around?

He pulled into a parking lot and unloaded camping chairs and a stout black bag with old sand stuck to it.

"You've had these chairs in your trunk this whole time?"

"That's where I keep them," he said, throwing his arm around her. "You never know when you're going to be on an unplanned vacation with your new girlfriend and get invited to a beach party."

She loved being referred to as his girlfriend, but it made her even more nervous about spending the next few hours among his friends, who were strangers to her. It also forced her to face – and then quickly tamp down – the question of how they could be together long-term.

He handed her the black bag.

"What's in here?" she said, dusting off old sand with her palm.

"Matkot."

"What's that?"

"You'll see."

Forty-five minutes later, they were enjoying campfire-roasted corn at a picnic table surrounded by fifteen people, some of Noam's friends and friends of friends. Six others played Matkot – a form of paddleball – half on the beach and half ankle-deep in the lake water. Everyone at the rave was friendly to Chelsea but not overly so, talking and joking with each other in Hebrew unless speaking directly to her.

"Here," a woman named Merav said, handing her a set of tongs and five foil-wrapped potatoes and guiding her with a gentle hand toward the campfire. "Can you help?" she asked.

"Oh, sure," Chelsea said happily since it gave her something to do amidst the conversations going on around her that she couldn't participate in.

"Israel is nothing if not egalitarian," Noam said as he approached the campfire himself, handing her a cold bottle of Prigat juice. "Even visitors pitch in."

"I like it," Chelsea said, kneeling down and placing the potatoes onto the fire with the tongs, turning them every few minutes.

Along with Merav, they sat silently watching the Matkot games, shifting seats whenever the wind blew cigarette smoke towards them. A few minutes later, David began singing and within two notes the whole crowd joined in.

"Tetaaru lachem olam yafe...."

In between verses, Noam whispered, "It's a famous song by Shlomo Arzi. The first lines mean, 'Imagine a beautiful world.'"

Merav was friendly – she smiled a lot and put her arm around Chelsea's shoulder, swaying as she sang – but she didn't speak much to Chelsea. If this party occurred in Colorado Springs, everyone would be chatting up the lone foreigner, asking where she was from, her favorite parts of the trip. Even Austin, someone who didn't always take to people who were "other," would probably have treated a foreigner with zoo-animal fascination.

"That's very American of you to notice," Noam said as they drove home. It was well past midnight. Chelsea's eyes burned from the cloud of cigarette smoke that hovered over her the last few hours. Her hair smelled of campfire.

"What do you mean?"

"Israelis aren't really into tiny talk."

"Into what?"

"Tiny talk – you know, chit-chat?"

She laughed. "*Small* talk."

"Whatever," he said, waving a hand playfully. "Many things my mom would call 'social graces' seem superficial to Israelis. Plus, most of those guys are insecure about their English."

"Really?" she said, surprised.

"Not everyone here has a Texas-raised mom like me." He looked up and re-adjusted his rear-view mirror. "They might have seemed brusque, but everyone definitely liked you."

Chelsea thought about the departing hugs she received from his friends, most of whom she hadn't even spoken to. But she knew a genuine hug when she received one. She needn't have been nervous about the night. In the strangest way, the gathering on an Israeli beach reminded her of the lunches in the Pulpit Springs social hall. It had the same qualities she loved about Sundays at church: the conviviality, fellowship and togetherness, if not the familiarity.

She leaned her head on his shoulder as he drove and meant it when she said, "I liked them too."

Chapter Twenty

He woke to find her reading. She was always reading. The New Testament or devotionals first thing in the morning, a novel at all other opportunities. She was two-thirds through *Marjorie Morningstar*, a nearly six-hundred page story (he'd checked) that she'd begun only about a week ago. Noam had never seen anyone read so much, not even Ronit's husband, whose actual job it was to study Torah. It meant that much of the time she was sitting still. He felt sometimes that he could paint her as a still life. Even when he was at work concentrating on complex data about gangliosides, Noam was moving – a finger through his hair, a foot rolling from left to right. Chelsea's ability to sit, moving only her eyeballs across a page mystified him. She walked fast, like an American, but she also could be still. He wondered if it was her church upbringing that enabled her to be rather than move or do. Or maybe it was her faith itself.

Noam had slept well. In his case, sleeping at all meant sleeping well. But with her, the heart-pounding jolts of fear as he slipped into unconsciousness nearly ceased. He didn't know if it was her presence itself or the nighttime ritual they'd begun. They'd make love – which could last mere moments due to lust or sometimes hours due to their mutual desire to prolong the lovely release that arose from their flesh touching. Afterwards, she rubbed lavender oil on him. She'd brought in her toiletry bag a collection of essential oils – lavender, frankincense, peppermint – that she'd purchased from a high school friend whose side job it was to sell oils the way housewives from the seventies sold Tupperware. She explained to Noam that many of her friends – new mothers, bored military wives – earned extra money this way. As a result, Chelsea had collections of everything from scented candles to skin care products to monogramed makeup bags to makeup itself. The oils, she explained, were one of the few products like this that she actually used. The evening after she told him about Austin, he'd told her more about somniphobia, confessing his phobia of slipping unmoored and vulnerable into unconsciousness. She hugged him and then quietly retrieved her bag of oils, massaging lavender oil into his scalp, on his chest and behind his ears. The earthy, floral scent, her touch, it careened him into the deepest, non-terrifying sleeps he'd had in months.

Now awake, he rolled towards her and stroked her shin as she read. "A novel? In the morning?" he said.

"I've been awake for awhile. I finished bible study already." She didn't look up from the page.

"Does your grandmother know you're almost done, that she should send you something else quick?"

Chelsea let the book fall on her thighs and looked over at him. "What?"

"Your grandmother – she sends you all these books. You might want to let her know that you're whipping through this one."

Sorrow and longing traveled over Chelsea's face. "My grandmother died."

"She – what? But you said she sends you all these books."

"She does. I mean, she arranged to have them sent to me." Her eyes glistened as she spoke. "She gave me book recommendations from the time I was a little girl. *The Black Stallion. A Tree Grows in Brooklyn.* All her favorites. I was a voracious reader, as was she, and we had the same taste in stories. Several years ago, when she was ill and knew that she was dying, she made arrangements with her favorite bookstore to send me books at oddly irregular intervals. I believe I'll be reading her recommendations until I'm as old as she was when she died. The first one that arrived after she passed away was *Anna Karenina*, which is partly why it's my favorite."

"That's remarkable." He thought about his own grandparents. He certainly loved them. But they were so different from him – his mother's parents from Texas, his father's European parents. Growing up, he'd seen each set about once a year. He loved being with them, gorging on barbecued ribs, tossing a Frisbee on a beach in France. But he didn't have this kind of shared passion with any of them.

"I know. I'm lucky. I still feel connected to her this way. It's also uncanny how her recommendations align with what's happening in my life."

"From what you've told me about *Eat Pray Love* and *Marjorie Morningstar*, I understand. Remarkable."

Forty minutes later, they wound through the elaborate breakfast buffet at Hagoshrim, a former kibbutz turned hotel in the Golan Heights with spacious grounds, bungalows, low-lying hotel buildings and a three-star restaurant. They brought their plates, piled high with quinoa-kale-favabean-egg-white omelets, to a small outdoor table.

"I like this hipster food," Noam said as he unrolled cutlery from a napkin. "But my all-time favorite breakfast is at a place in Texas my cousins always take us. It's an American – how do you say? – roadside diner. And that's what I love about it – it's so American. It smells of grease. The servers wear uniforms and you order from big plastic menus with specials printed in red. They bring you weak coffee in thick white mugs and heaping plates of hamburger, fries, pancakes and pies."

There was something more, Noam knew. That diner evoked a simplicity, a small life that strangely appealed to Noam. He, of course, knew better. He knew that life in the States could be harried and stressful. But always in that roadside diner, life felt predictable and contained, markedly less complex than the volatility of the Middle East. He imagined Chelsea's life in Colorado Springs as equally small and it was part of what intrigued him.

"We've got tons of those in Colorado. They're usually along highways."

"Exactly. They reek of loneliness and isolation but also, weirdly, of comfort." He paused, wondering when the next time he'd visit one of those diners was. And whether, in any possible scenario, he could be there with Chelsea.

"Do you mind if we pray before we eat?" she said, her honey hair shimmied in the morning breeze.

"You're welcome to."

She looked slightly stung and he urged himself to curb both his bluntness and, if it were at all possible, his agnosticism.

"Thank you, Father, for this lovely hipster food," she paused a beat, waiting for his appreciative laugh, which came, "and for this day in the Golan Heights, for my companion. In Jesus' name, Amen."

"You never asked to pray before."

"I've been a little distracted," she said, smiling just enough to show the beginnings of her crooked tooth. "But I want to continue to be me while I'm with you. Does it make you uncomfortable?"

"Not any more than when my sister and her family say hamotzi before eating."

"What's that?"

"Baruch Atah Adonai, Eloheinu Melech haklam, Hamotzi lechem min haartez. Amen."

"They end the same. What does it mean?"

"Literally, it means, '*You are blessed, God, our lord, king of the world, who takes out bread from the land.*' But really it means more – it reminds us of the privilege of having food to eat and connects an ordinary meal with faith in a future time when everyone will have enough to eat, free of the backbreaking work required by most just to put food on the table."

"Wow. Kind of heavy."

"We're Jews. We're funny but we're not lighthearted. There's a joke that every Jewish holiday is the same: 'They tried to kill us. We survived. Let's eat.'"

She didn't laugh. "When you first said that prayer, it made me think that Jews and Christians are more alike than not. But now, I don't know. I'm starting to see what you mean about the Jewish sensibility. It's not something that can be experienced by anyone who is not Jewish." Her expression was worried. It was an expression, Noam thought with irony, that some might characterize as Jewish.

"Everyone sees the world through a...wait," he said, thumbing through the translation app on his phone. "Through a prism. Is that how you say? Not a lot of vowels in that word. Anyway, I'm not an observant Jew but my prism is Jewish. Israeli and Jewish."

He noticed her plate still full of food. She'd hardly taken any bites, which was unusual.

"However you practice it – or don't – Judaism is a shared experience," he continued. "There's this unexplainable connection – we can spot each other in Thailand, in Buenos Aires, in New York City. We've all suffered. It's quite literally in our DNA. So we've got this built-in empathy – for the oppressed and the unfortunate."

She nodded. "My prism is a Christ-follower. An American."

"My prism has other angles too," he added. "I see the world as a scientist, as a painter too. And as a Dove – the empathy thing and all that."

"We've already determined I'm a Hawk." She placed her napkin on top of her barely touched plate. "Sometimes I feel as lost as last year's Easter egg. I guess I'm still figuring out my other angles."

》》》》》》》》》》》》》》》》》》》

THE BANAIS WAS ONE OF NOAM'S FAVORITE NATIONAL parks. He'd hiked its trails, woven among streams, since he and Ronit were kids. He wanted to show it to Chelsea not only because of its natural beauty, but because Yakov had told him that it was a place significant to Christians. According to their belief, it's where Peter identified Jesus as the Messiah. On the drive from Hagoshrim, Noam's phone rang several times, but he silenced the calls with a quick press of the finger. Work, he knew, was calling. He had no fewer than four clinical studies to evaluate, a weeks-long job that he'd now need to compress into days. Time, it felt, was running out. Being with Chelsea – this dream of intrigue, exploration, connection and passion – would end. Behind his sunglasses, he rolled his eyes at his own dream metaphor. Dreams, for him, had been elusive. Until recently.

As soon as they stepped out of the car at the Banais, Chelsea was taking pictures with her phone, her pink tank top revealing defined biceps poking from her slender upper arms.

Scanning her first shots, a look of alarm crossed her face. "My phone says, 'Welcome to Lebanon.'"

"Don't worry, don't worry. What are you – Jewish?" he said, guiding her onto the middle of three possible trails. "I haven't smuggled you across the border. We're at the northernmost point that Jesus ever was – but we're still in Israel. Your phone carrier just doesn't know it."

The trail he'd chosen offered expansive views of the Golan Heights. Even though it was early fall, native wildflowers in bright reds and purples peppered their path. Still – always – they inhaled the scent of the Mediterranean Sea. Their locked fingers separated every ten yards as Chelsea halted to snap more photos.

"Praise God," she said, removing her phone from her line of vision and simply taking in the scene. They were about to cross an ancient Roman bridge. Beside them, a waterfall framed by dark green foliage and rocks as beautiful as sculptures created a soothing nature symphony.

Observing her visceral reaction, to thank God for a place he loved, filled Noam with discomfort. He wanted so much what she had – a force to thank, a nucleus around which to center his feelings about being alive. But he had not found it. As envious as he was about what she found in Christ, he could never abandon his heritage. Being a Jew, even an atheist Jew, was in his soul. It was akin to whatever made him different from Fernando, his parents' cat.

"I don't know how we could consider giving up this land," she said, with a hand tented over her eyes.

He laughed sharply at her Hawkish connection to Israel's borders. But it meant that she'd internalized so much of what he'd being showing her. "Who's this 'we' you're talking about?"

She looked up at him. "How does it feel to be a Dove who birthed a Hawk?"

He shrugged and resumed walking, but she pulled on his elbow, holding him back.

"And I've been wondering," she continued, "how can you possibly remain a Dove after Adi was murdered by an Islamic extremist?"

Hearing Chelsea speak Adi's name sent a sizzle through his midline. "Are you the same as the Christians who bomb abortion clinics in the name of Jesus?"

"Of course not."

He stared at the landscape and then back at her. "Hating all Arabs because of Adi...that's too simple. Responding to hate with hate is to accept a flawed premise."

She nodded solemnly. "Perhaps what everyone needs is more of God."

He thought about his struggles around faith since Adi was killed. "Is passion for God the solution – or the very problem?"

They stared into each other's eyes, not speaking. After a moment, a gust of wind took hold of Chelsea's hair and she turned to swoop it into a ponytail. They continued up the trail, silently admiring the walls and moats built by Crusaders and peering into a still operational flour mill and olive press facility. She stopped to text photos of the scenery to her sister in Guatemala.

Sleeping soundly the last few weeks had given Noam a clarity he'd not had in a long time. Being with Chelsea had brought up many memories of Adi. And his new clarity meant that the torture of losing Adi was no longer a fuzzy, vague sensation. Instead, that loss was now so vivid he could give it a precise form on a canvas. He was certain he could only endure that kind of agony once in his life.

Watching Chelsea's slim fingers pound away on her phone, Noam's heart spoke to him. He had fallen in love with her. But he desperately, desperately wanted not to be. It was already too painful to imagine returning to real life, to contemplate no longer being with her.

As he processed his dueling realities, she chatted wistfully about camping trips her family had taken at the base of the Colorado mountains. They trudged up a slight incline that, on the heels of his sad revelation, felt to Noam like a mountain. He'd hiked this trail a dozen times in his life. But right then he found moving forward almost Sisyphean.

Eventually, they turned around to begin the trek back to the car. He felt a tearing inside his chest wall, and he heard, almost from outside his body, his own clipped speech, the constraint in his voice. The head-versus-heart debate in his mind was cacophonous, as intense as arguments among cabinet ministers in the Knesset, as arguments between Hawks and Doves. When they returned to the trailhead, his mind settled on the clear, undeniable truth: that he must save himself from heartache.

Chapter Twenty-One

C helsea's feet throbbed from the water's heat, but it felt good so she slowly lowered her body further into the tub. They were back at Hagoshrim after the hike at the Banais. She was tired from the walk and the blazing sun. Noam, in contrast, pulsed with a jittery energy so he'd grabbed his swim trunks and headed to the pool.

On the drive back from the Banais, she'd felt for the first time an odd distance between them. He leaned his head to the left, away from her, and kept both hands on the steering wheel. It was the first time since they'd reunited in Jerusalem that he hadn't held her hand or rested a palm on her thigh as he drove. It left her with an uncomfortable but eerily familiar feeling. She recalled Keith, her boyfriend from sophomore year in college, her first love who she thought she might marry someday. They'd been inseparable nearly the whole year, taking as many of the same classes as they could, studying together every night, bingeing on the Back to the Future trilogy on weekends, first the whole films and then just their favorite scenes, over and over and over. Until March. In March, after discussing how they could live near – very near – each other junior year without actually living together (something neither of their devout parents would condone), after planning how often they could see each other during the summer when he went home to Seattle and she remained in Colorado, after Chelsea had pleasantly exhaled into her first significant relationship, Keith began pulling away.

It was subtle at first. He'd be uncommonly quiet during dinners at Ike's, "their" place since the first weeks of school. He'd beg off of their nightly library run saying he needed to meet with his study group. (When did he get a study group? she'd wondered). Finally, he announced that he'd landed a summer internship in Washington D.C., nullifying her unrefundable plane tickets to Seattle in mid-July. (When did he apply for an internship in D.C.? she'd wondered.) At the end of the quarter, right before spring break, he'd called her from his last final exam, knowing that she still had two more to go, including the dreaded Chemistry final, and declared bitingly, "Just calling to say that I'm done and you're not." After her last exam, she broke up with him, not because she wanted to but because he'd left her no choice. Her parents' marriage was rather patriarchal, to be sure, but her father was never mean to her mother.

Noam hadn't been mean either. Before leaving for the pool, he'd squeezed her hands and looked her squarely in the eyes as if searching for answers. He was such a questioner – relentlessly asking how she knew for certain that Jesus was the son of God, asking how she knew the Bible was the word of God rather than simply a fascinating history book, and asking the hardest question of all: whether she believed that Austin, after what he'd done, was really a Christian. His questions were stimulating but also exhausting. It was something she loved – yes, loved – about him. He sought answers. She teased him that perhaps he should join the middle-aged, dark-clothed men they spotted in cafes and hotel lobbies, arguing animatedly about the meaning of ancient Jewish texts. There, in the room at Hagoshrim, she'd studied him back, his hotel-issued pool towel thrown over his shoulder, his light eyes appearing endless, like God's.

Noam wasn't anything like Keith but nonetheless she sensed the beginnings of a painful withdrawal, akin to those subtle shifts she'd first noticed in Keith that March so many years ago. In the tub, she swirled hot water around her body and then used her hands to bring palmfuls to her face. She washed away the grey-brown dust from the Banais paths. She cleansed between her toes. Twenty minutes later, the water began to cool, which was both a relief and a disappointment. She rose from the tub and pulled a plush towel around her, suddenly feeling overcome with exhaustion. She made her way across the tiled floor to the bed, and cocooned herself in the towel, naked underneath.

Moments after shutting her eyes, her phone rang. It was Crystal. She didn't feel like talking – to her best friend or to anyone. But she calculated the time difference and grew concerned that Crystal was calling from Colorado before dawn so she answered.

"Mama put me on the case," her friend announced.

"What do you mean?"

"Your mom is concerned about you. She called me. She says you ditched your tour group and are gallivanting around God's country with a strange man."

"Isn't it, like, barely five in the morning there?"

"I have babies, Chels. At this hour, I'm practically ready for lunch."

Chelsea couldn't help but smile. Crystal was living the life they'd both always wanted. And Chelsea was lying on a bed in the Golan Heights wondering if the Jewish man she'd fallen in love with but barely knew was about to break up with her.

"Seriously, though, what's going on with you?"

"Nothing." She could hear a baby gurgling.

"Are you still on the tour?"

"Not exactly. I mean, I'm still touring Israel but I'm not with the original group."

Chelsea looked around the room, at the deep brown tile floor, at the chairs and the drapes, which mimicked the colors of nature just outside their room. The places Noam had brought her had so much more spirit and personality than the generic Hyatts and other accommodations Christian Holy Land Journeys had arranged. With Noam, she felt both completely at home and yet like a foreigner.

"Didn't you spend your last dime on this trip?"

Chelsea's heart pumped blood upwards into her neck and face. She rolled onto her back and covered her eyes with her hand. "I did. I'm still on the trip. Just in a different way." She thought about the places she'd missed by abandoning the tour – Bethlehem, the Church of Multiplication, Capernaum. And then she recalled all the places she'd seen that she'd never planned to: Mary's Well, the tomb at Amuka, Yad Vashem, the Banais, the tiny Arab restaurants that Noam, a Dove, felt a principled need to patronize despite the fact that an Arab killed the girlfriend he loved. Every night, he'd study the now tattered copy of the Christian Holy Land Journeys itinerary, explaining how he'd keep the spirit of her intended journey and still show her his Israel.

"So it's true? You're with some man?"

"He's not 'some man.'" She felt defensive and protective, not sure she could even properly express her relationship to Noam. But what *was* he to her? Were they in a different time and space – say, in the US after meeting at a fellowship event in Colorado Springs – she'd unquestionably characterize Noam as the person she'd been waiting her whole life for. Austin? He'd been a mistake, a detour on the road to the man God had planned for her all along. She couldn't imagine two men more different: one spineless and robotic, the other expressive and principled.

The gurgling in the background turned into a full blown cry. Chelsea pulled the phone farther from her ear, though Crystal remained unfazed.

"Okay," her friend continued. "I get it. You met a guy. An Israeli guy, a *Jewish* guy, according to your mom. Unlike her, I'll try not to judge. But I want to remind you what you told me before you left: you need this trip to set you right. You need to trust again in Jesus and the path God is leading you on."

Those words, that admonition unmoored Chelsea. She grew dizzy and nauseous. Lying face up on the bed, she dropped one foot over the edge and planted it on the floor to steady herself. Crystal's words jolted her back to reality, to the truth: this time with Noam, no matter how exquisite, was simply a delay, a distraction from the certainty of what lay ahead. Despite the weightless, warm feelings she'd experienced in the last weeks, she had to figure her life out: where to live, how to support herself, where to worship, which friends remained.

The baby's cry careened into her ear drum, and at the same time, she heard the unmistakable electronic click signaling that Noam had inserted his card key into the door. She both wanted to see him and didn't. She wanted to disappear into the phone and transport herself back to Colorado and the life she'd long planned. And yet she also wanted to bury her head into Noam's chest, to have another one of their marathon nights of discussions and lovemaking. She came to Israel for clarity but now was more confused than ever. This journey was to be about regaining her faith, to face the uncertainties of her future with the strength of Jesus in her heart. But there was one problem: she didn't know whether God was leading her towards Noam or away from him.

Chapter Twenty-Two

A late afternoon breeze settled on Noam's damp shoulders as he marched slowly from the pool. The chill was in sharp contrast to how he'd been feeling the past weeks with Chelsea by his side, keeping him warm in bed and in spirit. Everything about their time together was a contrast. From the way he looked at the Palestinian conflict to what he wanted to paint (abstracts! figures!) had shifted since he rescued Chelsea from the Hasidic men on the bus.

Because of Adi, he knew what he felt for Chelsea was love. But he also knew he simply couldn't have it. The obstacles were too great. Chelsea was beautiful and benevolent and soulful and intelligent and funny. But her life was thousands of miles from his. She was a devout Christian who read from the New Testament every morning, asked God to provide everything from absolution to a parking spot, and prayed before meals. He was a patriotic Israeli, a scientist, a realist who refused to give up agency over his life to some unproven higher power.

No matter how fantastic and intense, love was no match for those real and practical obstacles. He didn't believe in hackneyed maxims about love – "love conquers all" – or age-old stories about star-crossed lovers who succeed against all odds. His disbelief in those ideals was as intense as his skepticism of God and Creation.

And yet...

Imagining his life in Tel Aviv without Chelsea by his side produced an almost physical pain. He saw himself pouring over data at Statyst, going out at night in Neve Tzedek, spending Shabbats painting, visiting with his parents and Ronit's family, trying to sleep again on his own.... How could it happen? Without Chelsea, food would taste dull, the Mediterranean Sea would feel dry.

Her own struggles were real too. She needed to return home, reconfigure her life, find a place to live and a sustainable job, and attain some sort of peace with her father. Noam cared too much for her to even entertain the unthinkable idea of her staying in Israel. As much as he wanted to keep his arms around her, to weave her tightly into his life in Tel Aviv, to spend lazy mornings in bed with her, to meet her for lunch during work days, to bring her to a proper beach bonfire with all his friends, he knew it was impossible. Where would her Christian faith fit into that picture? It was like trying to force the wrong ends of a magnet together – an unseeable power pushed them apart.

Making his way through the grounds of Hagoshrim along winding paths, Noam was both resolute and quaking. It was akin to how he felt as a new IDF soldier – a staunch Dove learning to shoot a rifle, drive a tank and outsmart hostage-takers. He didn't like what he had to do then, but he did it anyway.

He entered Hagorshrim's main building. The din of retiree couples and young parents with strollers checking in sounded like it had been run through an electronic audio program, everything muffled and elongated as if he were in a tunnel. From the dining area off to the left, the smell of dill and olive brine, savory flavors he normally loved, hit him as unpleasantly sharp.

Noam continued his march, gathering strength with each heavy step. He tried not to think about how the last few weeks had made him feel. He tried not to think about how compassionate Chelsea's reaction was to his bizarre phobia, perhaps his biggest shame. He shoved from his mind the sleep-filled nights he'd spent with her, the seamless transitions he'd experienced to the oblivion of slumber. He'd get that back somehow without her – or not. How she made him feel, how good he was with her around wasn't the point. Real life was the point. Their differences could not be overcome. Better to end it now, while she still had time to resume her original plan, retracing Jesus's life with Christian Holy Land Journeys so she could return home with the faith she'd undoubtedly need to launch a brand new life.

And he had to rescue himself – he was drowning but hadn't fully drowned.

His steps slowed as he approached their room. He pulled the card key from the pocket of his swim trunks and took a breath before inserting it. Years ago, his life with Adi ended in an instant. One phone call and everything had crumbled. Now, with Chelsea, the fissure was anticipated and prolonged. Both were blindingly painful.

He walked through the short tiled hallway into the room. Chelsea lay face up on the bed, one foot planted on the ground, the pit of one elbow covering her eyes. Her other hand, holding her phone, rested on her chest. He loved the curves and lines of her body. He wanted to stop right there and sketch her, the flow of her wispy hair as it draped on the pillow, the way her delicate fingers hung in the air – like a ballerina's or like Mary's in Michelangelo's Pieta, the most magnificent piece of art Noam had ever seen.

At the sound of his footsteps, Chelsea turned and passed him a weak smile, one that told a complete, sad story.

She knew too.

"Hi," he said.

"How was your swim?"

"Nice. It's cooling off out there." He tossed his towel over the back of the desk chair.

"I can tell."

He sat on the edge of the bed. *Marjorie Morningstar* lay face down on her nightstand, the paint chip with shades of purple that she'd been using for a bookmark on top. He nodded towards it. "Did you finish?"

"Yes, last night."

"And...."

"After traveling to Paris seeking an extraordinary life, Marjorie decides to return home. She becomes a suburban mom after all, a religious suburban mom."

He nodded. Of course she does, he thought.

Shadows from the darkening sky dampened the light in the room. Despite the fading light, he could see a new sadness on her face, her expression matching his own feelings.

"Did you talk to someone from home?" he asked, pointing to the phone in her hand.

"Crystal. My mom put her up to it."

He nodded again. "Your family is worried about you, being here but not where you were supposed to be."

"Yes."

He reached over and grabbed the beaten up copy of Christian Holy Land Journeys' itinerary. "They're up here in the north now too. You could resume your trip with them."

Her chin began to quiver. They were so aligned, so in sync. It was apparent that she knew precisely what he was thinking without him having to say it. It was probable, he realized, that she had already come to the same conclusion. As magical as they were together, as perfect as the last weeks had been, this could not go on. They were too different to make it work. They must not prolong the inevitable.

Noam forced himself not to look away from her, forced himself to maintain a neutral expression, to pretend that his heart was not shearing. Stoicism would make this separation easier for both of them.

"Yes," she said. In that short reply, her voice caught and she cleared her throat in an obvious effort to cover up emotion.

He lay down next to her, wrapping an arm around her waist. Because of Adi, heartache was familiar to him. This time, there was no murder, but he knew he'd soon face stabbing physical pain and a longing so profound it would tear him apart just like a piece of shredded cloth pinned to a Jewish mourner's clothing during Shiva. He'd made it through once – he'd do so again, no matter how soul crushing.

Speaking few words, they danced around what was actually happening, making it the most superficial conversation they'd ever had. Yet it was the conversation with the most damaging consequences.

He nuzzled in closer to her, imprinting her form, her smell, her energy, her faith into his brain. This was something he hadn't gotten to do the last time he'd been with Adi. For this, amidst the heartache that was ripping through his sternum, he was grateful.

"Yes," he confirmed.

"The only thing more unthinkable than leaving was staying;
the only thing more impossible than staying was leaving.

– Elizabeth Gilbert, *Eat Pray Love*

Chapter Twenty-Three

They were quiet in the car as Noam drove the twenty-five miles to the Sea of Galilee hotel where Christian Holy Land Journeys was spending the second of three nights in the region. It was the first time that silence between them was awkward. Noam turned on the radio, as if to introduce a third party into the equation, making the quiet seem less loud. The station played rap music – *Hebrew* rap music – and Chelsea felt farther away from The Springs than she had the whole trip. Leaning her head against the window, she closed her eyes and feigned sleep, her own attempt at making the silence between them less pronounced. It was a struggle to shut out the marvelous scenery that had so inspired her, an effort to slow her breathing to match the pace of a truly sleeping person. Inside, she was jittery and inclined to short, shallow breaths. She wanted to throw herself outside the car and run – to sprint from this spot she'd landed in. She wanted to disappear, to hide under the cover of the beautiful Middle Eastern sky until she could somehow fill herself with resolve to move forward. She wanted to shake her head vigorously, to launch out of her brain forever the sad words they'd spoken to each other.

I cannot betray my God.

I cannot betray my heritage.

But there was little – no, nothing – to replace these thoughts of her time with Noam, these memories of the last few weeks, the love, the thrill and, now, the pain. She could not distract herself with past memories because all she saw there was the carefully plotted life in Colorado that had fallen apart. And she could not look forward because for the first time her future was uncertain – she had no way to support herself, no sense of who was still with her. It felt as if everything she'd gained in the last few weeks was lost, as if none of it had substance or meaning.

So she did the only thing she knew to do: pray.

Jesus, I welcome your love. Fill my soul with wisdom. Show me my next step. Give me courage, instill in me hope. Guide me with your message.

She shifted in her seat, still feigning sleep, to wipe a tear with her shoulder. As the music escalated, she quietly cleared her throat, attempting to remove its constriction.

Minutes later, she felt the car slow and heard Noam clearing his own throat. He tapped her lightly on the knee. How she longed to feel his strong grip, to have him hold her hand as elegantly as he held a paint brush.

She opened her eyes and gave him a wan smile. His own in return was just as dim. She looked at the high rise hotel they were parked before – it was ordinary, nothing like the places she'd stayed with Noam.

Without words, they got out of the car. He took her luggage from the trunk and started towards the hotel lobby.

"Wait," she said. "I...I've got it from here."

He paused, put down her suitcase and nodded. That's how it was between them – even with few words there was understanding. How was this not working? she thought, heartbreak bubbling from the depths of her body to its outer sheath. Tears, unhideable now, filled her eyes – and then his.

He enveloped her in his arms. She smelled his distinct smell, an aroma she wanted to drink, fearing she'd never smell it again anywhere. Wrapped in his large and gentle body, she felt his soul, his questioning, scientific, searching soul. She backed away first, a move of self-protection and of grace. In return, he spoke their first words of farewell.

"You," he said, his voice catching, "have changed me."

It was the most loving, romantic thing that anyone – Keith, Austin, her family – had ever said to her.

She choked out a response. "Same."

They clung to each other again, knowing that words were insufficient to salve the forming wounds. This time, he pulled away first, though he clutched one of her hands in his and used his other to stroke her hair.

"I wish you...I wish you everything you want in this life."

She squeezed his hand and nodded in reply, resisting the urge to throw her body back into his, to insist that they run together to her room so they could make love, so she could feel every part of him with her fingertips as they'd done countless times in the last weeks. She looked once more into the bluest eyes she'd ever seen and tried to smile through their mutual pain. He was so foreign and yet now, so familiar, like long lost family. She thought of their visit to Yad Vashem and the stories she'd read about families who reunited sometimes a decade after the Holocaust. How odd, miraculous, comforting and utterly jarring that must have been. Saying goodbye to Noam, returning to Colorado – nothing seemed right.

I cannot betray my God.

I cannot betray my heritage.

Finally, after what felt like both seconds and hours, she turned away and grabbed her suitcase. Back at Hagoshrim, she'd sliced her finger on the box of devotionals cards as she'd hurriedly packed her things. It throbbed as she gripped the luggage handle. Both the smallest cuts and the deepest cuts hurt the most.

How could God have led her to this place, this place of agony and longing?

She couldn't look at Noam again. Instead, she slowly squeezed her other hand, the one still holding his, and then let it go.

>>>>>>>>>>>>>>>>>>>>

UPSTAIRS IN HER NEW HOTEL ROOM, SHE BANDAGED THE cardboard cut and regarded herself in the bathroom mirror. Her cheeks were fuller than they'd been when she'd left Colorado Springs. She'd put on weight thanks to all the hummus, milky coffees, olive oil and ice cream. And something about the sea air made her normally limp hair full of body. She was pleased with both effects and thanked God for providing something pleasant to notice amidst the confusion and pain.

She stood before the mirror, not knowing what to do with herself. At check in, she'd learned that Christian Holy Land Journeys was on an all-day excursion to Bethsaida and wouldn't return until much later that night. She considered calling Baylee but decided against it. The last time they spoke, Chelsea got the feeling Baylee was falling for a fellow missionary. She was in no state of mind to compare notes about love. She wanted to lie down but it was too early to sleep. It was dinner time, but she wasn't hungry. Not even the most delectable tray of halva slabs could tempt her. She felt as if she'd never be hungry again.

She sat at the desk in the hotel room and stared at a generic print of mallard ducks. She didn't dare sit on the bed, for she knew she'd keel over and fall asleep. And if she fell asleep this early, she risked waking in the middle of the night when the darkness and the quiet hid nothing. She knew from the sleepless nights she spent after ending her engagement that being awake in the middle of the night meant she'd have to face demons and own up to questionable choices. Not again.

She considered pulling out her bible or her navy notebook, but patience and focus escaped her. She paged aimlessly through the hotel binder with the room service menu and emergency exit maps and then picked up the magazine underneath it. It was an Israeli magazine in English. She skimmed recipes for homemade shwarma and articles ranking the Mediterranean's best beaches. When she landed on the feature story, a huge spread titled "Avengers," which she wouldn't have even noticed before arriving in the Holy Land weeks ago, she paused.

According to the story, after the Holocaust, a small group of surviving Jews attempted a mass poisoning of former SS men held at an American prisoner of war camp. Two thousand Germans were sickened but no one was killed, most likely because the poison was spread too thinly.

"These avengers felt a deep sense of injustice after most Nazis simply resumed their regular life after the war," a World War II historian from England was quoted as saying. "But despite human nature's visceral desire for vengeance, most Holocaust survivors were too weary and devastated for that. Instead, they focused on simply rebuilding their lives and starting new families – that was revenge enough against a regime that worked so hard to destroy them." The story quoted another professor, who added that physical retaliation was not only "counter to Jewish morals and traditions," but would have virtually no impact given the sheer scope of the genocide.

Chelsea glanced up at the mallard duck print as recent memories of Yad Vashem and the Hall of Remembrance swirled behind her eyeballs. How had she not considered the instinct for revenge – and the restraint Jews demonstrated in not acting on it?

Just then, her phone trilled. From across the room, she could see the screen.

Austin.

Her heart burned. She'd meant to block his number but amidst the happiness with Noam, it had slipped her mind.

She dove for the phone, bringing her thumb to the off button, but then hesitated. She hadn't spoken to Austin in weeks. It felt like a lifetime. Once again, everything was upended. She swiped.

"Hello?"

"Chels! Thank you for answering."

Tears sprang to her eyes at the sound of his voice. It was her old life calling. She was now a different person from the one who'd broken up with her longtime fiancée and then booked a ticket to the other side of the world.

"Austin." It was part statement, part question. She had nothing to say.

"Chelsea, I miss you. I'm sorry for what happened. Please come home."

She thought about Christopher Belford. She thought about the Avengers.

"No." But what did she mean? She couldn't stay in Israel. Especially now.

"I'm sorry, Chels. I disappointed you, I know."

"Yes."

"How can I fix this?"

She slumped back into the desk chair. "I know you're sorry, Austin," she said, wearily but not unkindly. "You can't fix our relationship. But you can think – really think – about what you did. And hopefully you'll find someone else who makes you happy." Happiness. She experienced an abundance of that in her short time with Noam, more than she had in all her previous years. "Please don't call me again, Austin."

She hung up and not trusting him to honor her request, blocked his number. Just then, she heard a knock at the door. Her heart leapt, and blood drained from her face and then instantly rushed back up to her ears. Was

Austin actually here, behind the door, coming to retrieve her with his bare hands? Or maybe Noam was coming back for her? Oh how she wanted to see his face again, to feel his biceps as he hovered above her, to feel his hot breath in her ear. And yet, she also considered hiding – under the bed, in the closet, behind the curtains. She wanted to resist the passion she felt for Noam, whose beliefs were so foreign to her, whose background was as different from hers as an Eskimo's. She felt more alive with him than with anyone else on the planet and yet she had to protect herself from the impossibility of a life together.

Another knock. And with that, she knew. She could tell from the heaviness, the pattern and the tone of the knock – it wasn't Noam. She was at once crushed and relieved.

"Just a minute, please," she called, hurriedly blotting her face with a tissue.

At the door, a large woman wearing a hotel uniform smiled warmly at her.

"Hello, Ms. Brinker," she said with a British accent. "We've been holding this for you." She handed Chelsea a package. "Our apologies for not presenting it when you checked in."

Chelsea thanked the woman and took the package to the small table by the window. It was from the US.

How did she know? she wondered, as she had so many times before.

Inside the box was the next book from her grandmother. It was times like these that Chelsea knew – *knew* – that God existed. She wanted so badly to share this moment with Noam, not to convince him to believe but to show him why she did.

This new book was *The Thorn Birds*, one that Chelsea had only a vague knowledge of. She read the back cover: "The heart of this sweeping, magnificent story of three generations in Australian sheep country is an ill-fated love affair. Father Ralph de Bricassart, a handsome Roman Catholic priest, must choose between Meggie Cleary, the woman he loves desperately and passionately, and the Church he has sworn his life to."

How, Chelsea wondered again as her body heaved sobs, *did she know*?

Chapter Twenty-Four

*W*hat had he done?

Noam asked himself over and over as he wound his car through the roads of the Galilee after leaving Chelsea at the hotel. He needed to get back to Tel Aviv, to reenter once and for all the life he'd abruptly abandoned. It was a life without Chelsea, but it was *his* life. His job, his apartment, his artwork, his family, his friends, his daily rituals. Everything for Noam was in Tel Aviv. Still, he ignored the increasingly irritated texts from Gil at Statyst. He needed to get back but he also needed time, a buffer between the spectacular and confusing weeks he'd spent with Chelsea and the familiar back in Tel Aviv.

As the Middle Eastern sky grew dark from Iraq to Jordan to Israel, Noam drove. He traveled north to the Hula Valley, towards Syria, where marshland around a lake was drained in Israel's early years to allow for sustainable agriculture, nothing less than an engineering triumph. He'd been to Hula Lake Park many times with Gil, an enthusiastic birdwatcher, because it had become a major stopover for birds migrating from Europe to Africa. But Noam didn't stop there this time. He continued driving, back through the Golan Heights, passing water towers and concrete structures built by the Syrians before the land was annexed by Israel. He continued, winding up two-lane roads, traveling higher and higher until he reached Mount Hermon, Israel's only ski resort. Noam had been there only twice – he never felt secure with skis or a snowboard beneath his feet. Now it was autumn, and the parking lot was full of outdoors lovers winding down the day after exploring the resort's biking and hiking trails. Reaching the highest point on the mountain with his car pointed northward, and with no where else to go, Noam turned off the engine.

Never had he been so unsure of a choice. At work, he relied on irrefutable data to guide decisions. When he sketched and painted, he regarded what was right in front of him, shadows and lines and bisected light. Precision, reliability, the ability to test and retest, those methods drove Noam's life. Even the anguish of Adi's death had a linear quality. She'd been the victim of senseless terrorism, but he never railed against the devastating fate. He accepted the horrific facts and slogged through his mourning. Even in those hardest times, he turned to science, reading books about the process of grief, mentally checking off the stages as he passed them.

During the worst days, those days when he thought he might split open from missing her, Noam tried to turn to spirituality. On Ronit's urging, he went to shul one Friday night. His mother accompanied him to Bet Asher, a reform synagogue in northern Tel Aviv that was akin to the Texas temple of her youth. At first, he actually felt some relief. He'd spent the days since Adi's death rushing – rushing to the hospital, rushing to be with her family, rushing to craft a eulogy that would convey the love he felt for her, rushing off the phone reporters who called asking for a statement, rushing to get back to work, to submerge himself in something other than heartache. So being in the synagogue just sitting, with his mother's shoulder resting against his, was comforting. But within a few minutes, as other worshippers chanted prayers together, that otherness he always felt in religious services returned. Noam and his mother stood when the rabbi indicated they should and sat when the rabbi pressed the air down with one

palm. He whispered along as they read from the prayer book. V'ahavta et
Adonai Elohecha, b'chol l'vavcha uv'chol nafsh'cha uv'chol m'odecha.
*You shall love Adonai your God with all your heart, with all your soul,
and with all your might.* Though he was outwardly in sync with the others
there, Noam's voice became progressively softer as he grew more isolated
from the worshipping around him. Eventually, feeling his mother's gaze
of understanding, he looked over and nodded. Together, they walked out.

And yet, Noam couldn't help but be envious of Chelsea's religion,
how it soothed her and guided her. He imagined that in that very moment,
if she was feeling even a fraction of the heartache that he was, that she
was turning to Jesus for consolation. Even more remarkable to Noam was
that she was likely getting that consolation. He wished that for himself, he
wanted that. But even if Jesus Christ were proven to be a real person who'd
actually lived, Noam would never believe that he'd been resurrected, that
he died on the cross for all of humanity's sins, that he was the son of God.

Even having this conversation within himself made Noam shudder.
Millions – millions – of Jews had died for sharing his heritage. Ancient
Egypt. The Spanish Inquisition. Pogroms. After the most horrific persecution, thousands of Jews fought, many with their lives, to give him Israel,
this place he loved so much. He did not read Torah. He did not know
whether God existed. He didn't believe that the Messiah would come. But
he cherished his heritage. The heritage that dictated that education – including teaching children to swim – was the chief parental duty. The heritage
that celebrated life, not an afterlife, even instructing that if a funeral and a
wedding were scheduled at the same time, Jewish philosophy demanded
the wedding be attended. The heritage that produced Lenny Bruce and Elie
Wiesel. Noam could not alter his primal feelings – he cherished hearty,
dark pumpernickel, not white bread.

Looking down on the Golan Heights from his parked car, Noam
had never felt so empty in a place he loved so much. He reached around
to the back seat and pulled a sketchbook from his bag. He began creating

an abstract doodle, the kind of loose, aimless sketch he'd begun drawing since meeting Chelsea. But he quickly found himself uninspired. He turned to his left and sketched the ski lodge with its seventies architecture. After a few minutes, he held the paper an arm's length away and discovered that even his realistic work, which he was so practiced at, had become flat. He tossed the sketchbook to the back seat.

He stretched his legs and closed his eyes. His mind returned to Chelsea. He imagined her life back in Colorado, nestled amidst mountains that were beautifully white-capped all year long. He pictured her working on marketing projects at the hospital, making a meal after work, settling into a night at home. Her weekends, she'd described, were filled with church volunteer work and social events and church itself. Her family, her friends, everything revolved around that. Life there held few surprises. Her manner, her way of life, her very soul exuded a straightforward ease that he craved, that calmed him. He recalled the hours of sleep he'd gotten in the last weeks – the kind of deep, restful, restorative sleep that had eluded him for years.

But then he reminded himself that correct choices are often the hardest. It was not easy for Eastern European refugees to leave everything – and everyone – behind to travel to Israel in the forties. It was not easy to live in British internment camps sometimes for years on end. It was not easy to defend Israel against attack from five Arab armies moments after declaring independence. Those choices weren't easy, but to Noam they were correct.

He picked up his phone, ignoring the text alerts from Gil and others at work. He'd return to Statyst tomorrow and would deal then with analyzing the metabolic changes in gangliosides resulting from new variables. He hit one button, his urge to call surprising him. After just two rings, Ronit answered.

"Everything is fine," Noam said, as if by rote, and then qualified. "Actually, I'm having a hard time."

He unloaded everything, recalling for his sister the last weeks, beginning with meeting Chelsea on the bus. As he spoke, he felt both heavy and light. He told Ronit about Chelsea's navy bible journal, her American phrases like "I was surprised as all get out," her addiction to cinnamon hard candies. When he described her faith, her love of books, how connected he felt to her at Yad Vashem, his voice caught. The emotion embarrassed him. Ronit didn't say much, but he could feel her affection, which surprised him. She could be judgmental not only about gentiles but also about non-observant Jews like him. But she offered quiet "tell me more" urgings.

"I love her, Ronit. Not just because she's beautiful and sexy. She has something...I can't explain it. It's something that you have too – a serene, radiating heart, a deep sense of spirituality," he said. "I want that too – so much – but I don't know how to get it."

She murmured in warm understanding. "Faith," she said, "isn't something you can 'get,' like you get a challah from the bakery on Friday afternoon. But her heart...maybe you can get that."

Chapter Twenty-Five

*I*n Tabgha, at the northwest corner of the Sea of Galilee, sit two churches: the Church of the Multitudes and the Church of the Primacy of St. Peter. The first is where Jesus is believed to have performed the miracle of the loaves, feeding far more people than the food supply would logically provide, and where he appeared after resurrection. The second is where Jesus is believed to have come to the apostle Peter, bestowing the primacy of the church on him.

When Chelsea first considered traveling to the Holy Land, Tabgha was a place she couldn't wait to see. The miracle of the loaves was perhaps her all-time favorite bible story. As a child, she'd listen to sermons about it, read illustrated books about it, watch bible cartoons about it. She turned the story over in her head thousands of times and imagined the disciples watching the miracle unfold. Sometimes it brought tears to her eyes.

But although Tabgha was on today's agenda, Chelsea felt more burdened than eager. The return to Christian Holy Land Journeys had been awkward. Kathleen had greeted her with a stiff hug and an enthusiasm in her voice that didn't match her expression. The other members of the group, who'd spent the last weeks forming bonds, mostly ignored her.

Ponytailed Matthew tried to strike up a conversation at breakfast but Chelsea kept her eyes pointed downward to shield him from the tears that hovered in her eyeballs. Eating oatmeal, talking with a man like Matthew, who was so similar to the men she'd grown up with, felt utterly beige compared to how she'd felt with Noam.

Like everyone else, Chelsea returned to her room after breakfast to freshen up and get ready for the visit to Tabgha. She sat on the bed absently peeling back corners of the worn stickers on her laptop and considered staying in her room for the day. She'd spent hours the evening before looking for new jobs in Colorado and even researching the cost of living in other cities. She still couldn't imagine the pain of trying to resume everyday life in The Springs. In a fit of absurdity and defeatism, she even considered Alaska before abandoning the search altogether in favor of reading *The Thorn Birds*.

As productive as more planning and research would be, returning to the tour only to remain in the hotel seemed the height of both rudeness and stupidity. It was one thing to abandon the tour for a rare insider's look at Israel but it was another to abandon the tour to spend the day on the Internet. She could do that after the trip even if it meant holing up in her parents' house for a few weeks, staying as far away from her disappointed father as she could while she figured her life out.

In the bathroom, she used soap and water to remove sticker glue from underneath her thumbnail. She inspected the stud in her upper ear, which no longer surprised her. The skin around the new piercing was nearly healed. She leaned back and examined her face in the harsh fluorescent light. This time last week, she'd been basking in the tan acquired from the long walks outdoors she'd taken with Noam. She'd come to love wearing little or no makeup – he'd been right, she didn't need it. Today, though, she looked haggard. She considered lining her eyes, which appeared shrunken from crying, but didn't have time.

"Why has thou forsaken me, Lord?" she whispered and then rolled her eyes at her reflection. As confused as she felt, she also knew she was feeling sorry for herself. After her long discussions with Noam about prayer, she'd privately vowed never again to ask Jesus for something as ridiculous and earthly as less puffy eyes. It demeaned her – and Christ.

Kathleen seemed surprised and gratified to see Chelsea actually board the bus, the last one on before the elderly couples who used wheelchairs and walkers. Kathleen gave her a small nod of approval akin to the way a second-grade teacher might acknowledge a disruptive boy who'd finally gotten with the program. It made Chelsea want to run.

She found a seat towards the back of the bus and put ear buds in. She debated listening to the new album by King Mercy, a Christian band that Baylee and Crystal were obsessed with, or The Good Word podcast. But she didn't have the energy to scroll through her phone to find either. So she just kept the ear buds in, listening to nothing, and hoping it would dissuade someone from striking up a conversation as they drove to Tabgha.

About ten minutes later, Kathleen got on the loudspeaker and began relaying the history of the region, much of which Noam had already told Chelsea.

"We're getting towards the end of our tour," Kathleen said. "We only have a few more days together before we travel back to Tel Aviv and you all make your way home via Ben Gurion Airport."

Chelsea shifted in her seat. The thought of enduring airport security, waiting in line at the gate, sitting in the small coach seat for upwards of eleven hours made her very – or as Noam would say, she thought longingly, "very, very" – tired. The prospect of leaving Israel, probably forever, made her unspeakably sad, and she squeezed her eyes shut.

"In our last days together," Kathleen continued, "I hope you'll appreciate the massive contributions to civilization that have sprung from this tiny place. From Monotheism and the Scriptures to science, agriculture and the arts, Israel's contributions are remarkably disproportionate to its size. We must thank God for the blessings we enjoy because of what he has done through Israel – and the Jewish people. It is without question that God loves this complex Jewish state. We remember Deuteronomy: 'For thou art an holy people unto the Lord thy God: the Lord thy God hath chosen thee to be a special people unto himself.' For centuries the Israelites were scattered, but God remained faithful to the promise that one day they would be returned to this beloved place. Christ has protected the Israelites from extinction and used Israel to bring a savior into this world."

Chelsea glanced around. One woman was knitting. Another was fishing for something in her purse. Matthew was sleeping, mouth agape. Chelsea wanted to scream. Kathleen's words were the first she'd spoken that had meaning to Chelsea. This place, this Israel, it was magical. For Chelsea, it had produced not one savior but two. Though they were now separated and she'd likely never see him again, Noam had saved her somehow. He'd shown her that she'd deserved mercy for her mistakes. He'd shown her that there was a way to be soulful without being Godly. He'd shown her that the way of life she'd always known was lovely but also flawed, something both to envy and to question.

It was breezy when they arrived at the Church of the Multitudes. And despite six tour buses full of visitors, it was also exceptionally quiet. According to Kathleen, this spot at the foot of the Mount of Beatitudes, home to the Sermon on the Mount, was ideal for silent prayer and study. "It's why we put this site towards the end of our journey together," she explained as everyone departed the bus.

Despite the puffs of wind, Chelsea chose to stay outdoors rather than take the indoor tour of the church. It wasn't the structure itself that was important, it was what happened here. And she opted out of the chance to sail on a replica of Jesus's fishing boat. Instead, she found a concrete bench with a view of the Sea of Galilee. If Noam were with her, she'd insist he take out his sketchbook. The landscape was magnificent and she knew he could capture the ragged edge of the lake with expert swipes of his pen. She felt alone without him.

Staring at the sea, she imagined Christ performing his feat of multiplication, thousands upon thousands of Israelis being uplifted by the miracle. And she imagined herself there, waiting at the back of the line, hoping there'd be enough. That's how she always imagined it – with herself at the back of the line. And that's how she felt now – at the back of the line, waiting for God to remind her that he was there for her, that he had a plan for her, that he would provide for her. She pictured telling that to Noam, who'd insist – *insist* – that she was strong and courageous and could provide for herself.

Weeks ago, when she first learned that he was a non-believer – a Humanist – she felt sorry for him. Not only did he live this life refusing evidence of God all around, but he'd also spend eternity outside of Heaven without God then too. In those early days together, she'd wanted to convince him, to prove that he was wrong, to tell him that he simply had to *decide* to believe and he'd then reap all the benefits of faith. But now, she just wanted to be with him – in any way, in any state of belief or disbelief. She wanted to hold his hand, to watch him paint, to follow him around this magnificent country many times more, to meld her body with his. That desire was separate from belief, and yet part and parcel of it. God had brought her to Noam, who showed her a different way of being alive. Not better or worse – just new.

Another tour group – from Australia, based on their accents – gathered a few feet from where Chelsea sat. Their leader wore a large cross and spoke with a thick Israeli accent. A native Christian, Chelsea marveled.

"When you return Down Under," the leader said, "remember that we bring people to Christianity not by telling others that our beliefs are right and theirs are wrong. Rather, we simply live our lives with such a radiance that they are drawn to us, wanting to know for themselves the source of our light."

Chelsea lifted her chin skyward, stunned at the truth of the man's statement, a statement in sharp contrast to the proselytizing nature of the Christianity that she'd grown up with, in notable contrast to what her father and Austin had done – trying to prove their beliefs were right by shaming someone who didn't share them.

She wanted to slide into this group and hear more from their leader. She wanted to talk to a neutral third person, to seek guidance about the right path, the right next step for her.

Moments later, without warning, Chelsea felt emboldened, a restless fire brewing in her belly. In an instant, she knew – not because of God, not because of someone's demand, but because of her own heart – what she had to do.

The night before, while worming her way deep into *The Thorn Birds*, Chelsea had read about Aunt Mary presenting her niece Meggie and Father Ralph a seemingly impossible choice: love or the church. As Chelsea's eyes drooped while turning pages, she sleepily observed that the choice was simply false. Love and the church were not mutually exclusive.

On the bench in Tabgha, she thought more about Father Ralph. Wanting to be of service to God, he lived his life in pain, denying himself the opportunity to truly serve God by loving another person selflessly, just like Jesus did.

That truth hit Chelsea like a blast from Heavenly trumpets.

Chapter Twenty-Six

oam took a sip of wine and began unpacking the art supplies he'd purchased that afternoon. The wine was a merlot he'd bought days before in the Golan Heights. He was not accustomed to drinking alone or to opening a bottle of wine before it was ready. But this bottle was special. He'd acquired it on one the happiest days he could remember, a day he'd spent with Chelsea touring the Golan. Because of that, it would always be special – and painful. Better, he figured, to endure the pain of reliving those days through a bottle of wine now, while he was already lacerated. How much worse could he feel? he thought as he uncorked it. He inhaled the floral yet earthy scent and tried not to think about Chelsea's kind eyes and the energy and serenity she brought him.

Yes, better to endure this now, he thought, hoping the alcohol's numbing effects would dull the pain of the memories the wine itself conjured – like washing down aspirin with the champagne that caused the headache in the first place.

Noam could have given the bottle away. But in a twisted way, he wanted to reach rock bottom sooner. He knew from the anguish of Adi's death that the single benefit of being at one's lowest point was that there was nowhere to go but up. It was a truth as immutable as the Pythagorean Theorem.

With that goal in mind, he took another long pull from the glass and sorted his new supplies: brushes, sponges, sketch paper, canvases, and wooden sticks for nailing those precise edges. He fingered several small tubes of paint, sample sizes of colors he was not accustomed to – muddy, muted colors rather than the vivid primary colors he normally purchased by the liter. He had everything he needed to dive into the activity that never failed to shut everything else from his mind, except one last thing: a subject.

When he returned home from Galilee, he cleared his home studio of everything he'd previously planned to paint: food wrappers, tech gadgets, odd-shaped fruits and common bathroom items like toothpaste tubes. Those objects were no longer right. He'd mastered them. He considered painting loose and freeform, the way he'd begun doing in his sketchbook while with Chelsea, but abstracts didn't seem right either.

He walked around his apartment, sipping the merlot as he considered what to train his eye on for the next several hours. He went to the window and gazed down at the street below, considering taking his easel outdoors to try his hand at capturing the street scene. But he – and his process – would be exposed. Maybe someday he'd bring his supplies outside to paint the Mediterranean shore or the green hilltops at the Lebanon border. But not yet.

He turned away from the window and surveyed the living room. He came up empty. The wine was making him sleepy but he was not ready to endure that battle against sleep. The last few nights had been some of the worst: pulling himself from the brink of unconsciousness with panicked gasps. For days he felt like he was trying to reenter his life with an old key when the locks had been changed. He'd been changed.

He needed to paint. Beginning to feel like an addict who would soon need a hit to avoid sure disaster, he trudged through his apartment with increasing urgency. He marched down the hall to his bedroom and scanned the room from wall to wall. His eyes finally landed on what he knew instantly was the subject of his next still life: a stack of books.

Placing his wine glass on the nightstand, he knelt down to survey the open shelf beneath the table top. *A Prayer for Owen Meany*. (What kind of title was that?) *All Creatures Great and Small*. He'd only read one book from the stack of more than ten. Most had just been thrust on him by his mother, who went through books the way most people went through magazines. But Noam wasn't a big reader. Holding the books, he thought of Chelsea. In the weeks he'd known her, she'd read several novels. Painting a stack of books would have the same desired effect as opening the precious wine – it would accelerate the pain, push him closer and quicker to bottom.

Back in his spare bedroom, he spent several minutes arranging the books in an off-kilter pile with some bindings facing in and others out, with the smallest book in the middle rather than on top. The arrangement gave the books a quality of movement, an unsteadiness that mirrored Noam's emotional state. After several tries with a spotlight lamp, he finally nailed the lighting. Though he wasn't a bibliophile like his mother or Chelsea, he wanted to capture precisely the mystery and unpredictability of a good story.

He painted for several hours, immersing himself in the tedious task of creating perfectly straight lines on an angle, mixing the exact yellow-y beige color of page edges, hand-lettering titles as they appeared on the bindings. He took a bathroom break and as he was walking back across the hall, Noam heard the doorbell. It startled him. He'd been painting for several hours and felt he was on another planet rather than in his home. He crossed through the living room, remembering how for months after Adi died, every time his phone rang, his first thought was that it was her. Every time he said hello, he'd drop back into despair.

He swung the front door open but found the space in the hallway empty. Confused, he closed the door and stood in the living room. Then he heard the sound again. It wasn't his doorbell but rather the beeping of a delivery truck attempting a three-point turn in the street below. Noam trudged back to his studio.

»»»»»»»»»»»»»»»

HOURS LATER, HE WOKE TO POUNDING. AT FIRST, HE thought it was his head. He'd consumed nearly the entire bottle of merlot before dumping the last sedimenty bits down the drain. The wine had indeed brought him down the spiral he sought, but also disturbed his ability to paint. As the alcohol embedded itself to his cells, the accuracy and realism he strived for eluded him. Eventually, he tossed himself onto his bed – still in the splattered scrubs he wore for painting – and waited for his demons: Adi, unconsciousness, and now Chelsea.

The pounding grew louder. He sat up and realized it was actual pounding, not simply vessels pumping dehydrated blood through his skull. His joints popped as he rose and looked out the window. This time, the noise was not coming from outside.

More pounding. Then he heard a voice.

"Noam, if you're there, please open up."

He stumbled out of the bedroom, down the hallway, through the living room to the front door. When he opened it, there stood Chelsea. Her right palm was fisted and frozen in mid-air, poised to strike the door again. Her expression was one of surprise and then elation.

"Hi," she said. "I'm sorry to be so loud...I...." She moved her suspended arm awkwardly to her side. "Hi," she repeated.

"Hi." When he'd left her in Galilee, the thought that pierced his sternum more than any other: that he might never see her again. And now here she was.

"I see you've been painting." She pointed to his dingy, paint-splattered scrubs.

He ran a hand through his hair, wondering if he looked as hung over and disheveled as he felt. "Yeah, pretty badly. But yeah." He stood in the doorway looking at her. She wore jeans paired with sandals she'd bought at a small boutique in Safed, and a new earring, a small round hoop, in the new cartilage piercing. "Oh, sorry. Come in, come in."

He gestured to the couch, and she sat. He didn't know whether to sit or stand or how close to be to her. He knew how close he wanted to be, but he also knew that no matter how magical and soothing her presence, the same barriers remained. After a moment, he sat two cushions away.

"This isn't polite," she said, "coming here unannounced. I paid eighty-five shekels to a taxi driver to help me find your apartment. We started at Dallal and wove around every street within a three mile radius. It took forty-five minutes but I had to see you again."

Noam desperately needed a glass of water. But he was afraid to move. Even from his spot on the couch, he could smell her, her clean, jasmine scent with traces of the lavender oil she used to soothe him to sleep. It was a better balm for his body than anything he could eat or drink. And yet, he knew this moment of delight would catapult him up and then back to rock bottom, like a yo-yo that hovered above its tautest point before rolling back up. Rock bottom was agony but it was also the start of healing. Being here with her was delaying that. He remained silent.

She continued. "I've thought so much about what unites us, what separates us. I am more like you, a Jew, than I am like Austin, a Christian capable of deplorable acts. Or my father...." She looked away and took another breath. "And you're more like me, a Christian, than you are like the Hasidic men we encountered on the bus."

He nodded.

"I know you say you're a Humanist, but I'm not sure that's true. The difference between you and someone who believes solely in the power of man is that you are searching. You *want* to believe."

"Chelsea," he said, his voice sad. "I cannot believe in your God. I do not believe in Christ. I am a Jew."

She held up a hand. "I understand. I do. Have I ever proselytized Christ to you?"

He thought about her daily scripture study, the stack of devotional cards, the joy she exuded in her beliefs. Never once, though, had she tried to convert him. If anything, she'd asked questions about Judaism to draw out faith from his own traditions.

He smiled at the realization. "No, you haven't."

"I'm reading this book, a new one from my grandmother. It's a long, absorbing saga. I'm not finished but I hit this point where two people – two very different people who should not be in love but are – must make painful decisions. They're painful because the characters believe they have only two choices – this or that. But they don't."

He nodded, though he was unsure of her point.

"It made me realize that this beautiful, magnificent, complicated country has made you believe that you must be secular or orthodox. But it's a false choice. You can be anything."

"I cannot be a Christian."

She shook her head briskly. "I am not asking you to. Noam, you are one of the most soulful people I've ever known. You may not call it that. But I do. You're nonjudgmental, patient and benevolent. You're more connected to God – or the universe or whatever you prefer to call it – than you know."

He scooted centimeters closer to her, tears blurring his vision. It was the most moving compliment he'd ever received.

Her eyes, too, filled with tears. "Noam, you may spend your whole life trying to find the peace I've found in Jesus. You may find it elsewhere – in your God, in Buddhism, in nature – or you may never find it. But in the last few days, I realized that as long as I'm with someone who is trying to find it, who is searching, that's enough."

"I want to be more than 'enough.'" He thought about how whenever he was with religious people – Jewish, Christian, Muslim – he felt that he was missing out. His whole life had been about wanting to understand, to know, to have proof. But perhaps, he thought, he could be, if not a believer, then a definitive seeker, and selecting that option was a faith of sorts itself.

Chelsea leaned into him, gently moving his hair behind his ears, and he felt a release in his psyche, a pleasant succumbing. She kissed him gently on each cheek and then brought her nose to his. "Noam, since I've been without you, as I've re-read scripture and visited holy places, I've determined with a certainty I've never felt before: you are enough and much, much more. You are my beshert."

Chapter Twenty-Seven

Chelsea's body grew at once taut and jelly-like as Noam clung to her. She fingered his black hair, her irises burrowing into his. Within seconds, they were panting, unclear whose furious breaths were louder or quicker. Though they wanted to rush, to satisfy their urges, by some tacit agreement emblematic of their connection, they forced themselves to move slowly. She moaned as he unhurriedly lifted her shirt over her head and then lightly traced her nipples with his strong fingers.

"Now," she wanted to shout as her body prepared for what was to come. But she bit her lip and let the slow dance continue. One by one, she removed his clothes and ran her palms over his body, leaving a centimeter of air between them. Eyes closed, mouth parted, he shook almost imperceptibly.

After she removed all his clothes, he gently laid her down and separated her legs – placing one on the top edge of the couch, the other on the floor. He positioned himself between them and began gently stroking her nipples again. Whimpers escaped her and the scent of the passion between them filled the air. He brought a hand between her legs and spread every part of her, expertly sliding his fingers up and down. Soon, she felt herself moving her hips to match the rhythm of his hands and she heard her own breathless, animal sounds and his own "ohhhh." Through barely open eyes, she could see the erotic thrill he got from pleasuring her, and in that moment her eyes rolled skyward and her body quaked. He continued to touch her as she climaxed, slowing his pace and knowing precisely when to stop. Her breath still quick, she grabbed his biceps to bring him on top of her. He was stiff and pulsing as she guided him into her. When he slid to the farthest points of her body, they cried out in unison. He moved slowly at first but he soon quickened his pace and exploded as involuntarily as she had moments before. Feeling this, her own body quaked again, surprising her. She pressed her fingertips into his lower back as they moaned together again. "Ohhhhh," they cried. "Ohhhhhh."

>>>>>>>>>>>>>>>>>>>>>>>>>

UTTERLY SPENT, THEY SLEPT ON THE COUCH FOR WHAT seemed to Chelsea like hours. When the sun poked through the blinds and hit their entangled bodies on the couch, she opened her eyes. She relished the soft sound of Noam's quiet snoring, knowing that sleep was, for him, hard-fought. She stroked his head the way one would a beloved, aging pet and took in his earthy smell. They lay like that for another long while before Noam finally stirred.

"Thank you for coming to me," he said, brushing hair from her forehead.

His breath on her face, warmth traveled up her spine. "I couldn't stay away," she said. It was true. His pull over her was magnetic. Now that they'd experienced the joy of their unique connection, life would never be the same. She knew that.

"So what do we do now?" he said.

She propped herself up on one elbow, looking down at his face, covered in stubble. "I'm not sure that I can be without you."

He closed his eyes and nodded, a grin forming on his lips. "Me too," he said, kissing her bare shoulder. "But, I repeat, what do we do now?"

"Always blunt, always practical," she teased and then sat up fully, throwing the t-shirt he'd been wearing over her body. It covered her to the knees, making her feel dainty. "After you left Galilee, I could do nothing but think and pray. A truth kept announcing itself to me over and over. Something very special," she said, moving a hand back and forth between their chests, "has happened here."

He grabbed hold of her hand and squeezed it in agreement. A relief and elation settled over her, though her heart pounded as she prepared herself for the rest of what she had to say. Everything she'd rehearsed as she traveled south from Galilee to Tel Aviv escaped her brain, leaving her completely, wholly in the moment.

"I believe – I know – that God wants us to be together," she said. "You probably want some sort of proof but I can't give you a spreadsheet or the results of an experiment. You'll have to trust me. Or at least examine the evidence as you know it – the way we met, the closeness we feel despite our differences, the joy the last weeks have brought us."

He squeezed her hand again.

"There's more. While I was in Galilee without you," she said, "I learned of a job. A friend I used to work with in marketing at the hospital told me about an assistant marketing director job at the bookstore chain she now works at. She thought of me because of how much I love books. The salary – assistant director level rather than coordinator – is more than I'm earning now – not a fortune, to be sure, but certainly enough to support myself. The job is in Atlanta. That means I can have a fresh start in several ways – away from Austin, my parents, the life I grew up in. It's something I'm finally ready to do. This opportunity...it's another God miracle for us."

He cocked his head to the side in question. "How so?"

"I've only been to Atlanta once but it's pretty cosmopolitan for being in the South. It's no Tel Aviv but it's a big city with diversity. I did some research. Do you know the CDC?"

"Of course. Many of my reports are reviewed by the CDC and equivalents here in Israel and around the world," he said. Then he sat up in understanding. "The CDC...is in Atlanta."

"Right," she said, her speech quickening. "I know you can work remotely – I've seen you do it as we traveled. In between our eating world-class meals, showing me Israel's magical sites and," she smiled, "making love, you were able to work. You told me that when you traveled for a month in Thailand last year you worked then too."

"Ken."

"So," she asked, as hopeful as a game show contestant waiting to hear if she'd solved the puzzle correctly, "could you work in Atlanta? I mean, if not permanently at least for a little while?"

Noam was quiet, his expression neutral.

"I know you love Israel," she continued. "I love it here too. I don't know what the future holds – where you should live, where *we* should live. But I'm wondering about giving this – us – a real chance. I did more research. There are dozens of flights a day from Atlanta to Tel Aviv. Dozens. You – we – could return here frequently. And in addition to churches, there are dozens of synagogues there, reform, conservative, orthodox, even something called reconstructionist. I even watched one of the services online. I think you'd like the music. Even though it's in the Bible Belt, Atlanta also has mosques, Hindu temples and Tibetan Buddhist monasteries."

"Does that matter?"

By now, she'd learned not to take his Israeli brusqueness personally. "We know that it does for me. And if you're on your own journey of faith, going through the motions is a place to start. Maybe sitting in shul, enjoying the music, perhaps even making friends with people you meet in the community, maybe the beliefs will come. And even if faith doesn't come, doing those things is certainly not going to *hurt* anything. I'll even go with you. Maybe we can find friends together – after all, we'd both be starting from scratch there." She paused, trying to capture and express the intensity of her feelings – for him, for religion, for the new life she wanted to try. "Faith," she said, "is partly about letting go of what no longer serves us. It's about being open – to God miracles like the ones bringing us and keeping us together, open to being changed in ways that we can't even imagine."

Noam let out a small breath and she held hers, not knowing whether his response would thrill her or break her heart. The proposal was risky – for both of them. Until she spoke the words aloud, she hadn't been sure she could actually go through with it. Being together would disappoint others. By declaring their love, with no guarantee of how long it would last, they could lose their families. After what felt like a suspended hour, he smiled and hugged her, wordlessly approving of her plan. "I thought you were a 'low-risk' person," he said.

She brought her nose to his, convinced that this crazy, insecure path was worth it if it allowed her to live as her true self alongside Noam, their community of two. "You changed that."

He turned to the window, his eyes sparkling in the light. "So we're both going to upend our lives not knowing how it's all going to wind up?" He looked back at her and let out a small laugh. "Strangely, I'm okay with that."

She threw her arms around his neck. "That," she said, "is faith."

Chapter Twenty-Eight

*N*oam could smell his mother's roast chicken all the way from the sidewalk outside his parents' home.

"We're here," he said, opening the passenger door and extending his hand to help Chelsea out. She wore a simple yellow sundress and carried an enormous bundle of purple and red anemone flowers.

"I told you, it's really, really not necessary to bring anything," he said, guiding her down the front stairs. "To welcome anyone, including strangers, into your home is very Israeli. Ten years ago, a woman visiting from France knocked on our door. She'd looked us up in the phone book, certain that she and my dad were distant cousins. She brought a stack of black-and-white photos and a family tree. My parents invited her in, served her lunch, heard her whole story and reviewed her documents. It turns out, we weren't related."

"Yikes. My mom would have been madder than a wet hen."

"No, no, it was fine. In fact, we had a wonderful time with her. We still keep in touch. My parents even met her for dinner on a trip to Paris a few years ago."

"Wow," she said, slowing her pace as the sounds of conversation and laughter from inside grew louder. She looked at Noam uncertainly.

"I'm *saying*," he continued, wrapping his arm around her shoulder and leading her to the front door, "there's no need to be formal, nothing to be nervous about." He hoped he was telling the truth. Chelsea had already lost so much. A phone call to her parents the night before, explaining their plans, had ended abruptly. Chelsea's face had lost all color as she held the receiver with its audible dial tone. She'd been right all along about the life that she'd left, the life she'd long planned – it had vanished.

His mother opened the door as they approached.

"Welcome!" she said.

"Hello, Ima." He kissed her cheek and gathered her in a hug. He turned to Chelsea, who sported a nervous, zig-zaggy grin. "This is my girlfriend, Chelsea."

His mother opened her arms and grasped Chelsea, crushing the flowers but also relaxing Chelsea's strained expression. "Nice to meet you. Come on in."

"She oozes...warmth," Chelsea whispered to Noam out of the side of her mouth. "You weren't kidding about Israelis being welcoming."

"Israelis are welcoming, but my mom is American. What you're feeling," he said with pride, "that's simply from being Jewish."

Inside, Noam's father embraced Chelsea before even being introduced and then kissed his son on the lips.

"Aba," Noam said, "this is Chelsea."

"Come in, come in," his father said, ushering them into the sunken living room. "Let's see...who've we got here? That's Ronit, Noam's sister. And a few of her kids...Uri, Davi, Inda. The rest are in school or at shul with their father. Sit down. We're discussing what our sukkah should look like for Sukkot in a few weeks. Ima says she wants a 'beautiful' sukkah with flowers and twinkling lights, not a 'typical, utilitarian Israeli' sukkah that favors function over aesthetics."

Noam hadn't revealed to Chelsea that he'd been apprehensive about this gathering too. He hadn't introduced a woman to his family since Adi and certainly never an American woman or a shiksa. Aside from Ronit, his family wasn't religious, but he still didn't know whether they'd accept someone with such different beliefs. Within moments, though, his own uncertainty dissipated. Even Ronit, in her head-to-toe coverings, engaged Chelsea in friendly conversation. He remained willing to see how life together would unfold.

"Noam," his mother said. "Come with me to the office. I'd like to show you something."

He followed her upstairs. "What is it, Ima?"

"Oh, nothing," she said, plopping onto an old love seat his parents kept in their joint home office. She patted the spot next to her and he sat. Fernando the cat hopped onto Noam's lap. "I'm just being sneaky. I wanted to check in on you. How are things going? She's very pretty."

"Yes, she is."

"This is different for you."

"It is."

"You know, we Americans aren't so bad...."

Noam chuckled. "I know. She's wonderful, in all the ways Americans are wonderful. She's also Christian. I'm not Ronit, not even close, but I'm still a Jew in my bones."

She squeezed his hand. "I'm glad about that. Still, there's something about her...." She prodded.

He nodded. "As alien as it is to me, her faith is partly what draws me to her."

"It's so funny mothering a grown man. You're exactly the same as you were thirty years ago. You like things smooth, cut and dried. You see life as black or white. When you became a scientist? No big surprise."

He, too, recalled the days of believing that a school teacher was either good or bad, a person was a friend or not. It's why the army, though mandatory, appealed to him: procedures were clear cut. It's why he was drawn to realism in his art – the edges, the shadows, the shades of color – they were verifiable.

"I knew it would hit you at some point," his mother said, with a playful smugness.

"What?"

"Life is not black or white, Mister Fancy Scientist. It's grey. Think of Chelsea as the paint brush that combines the white and the black on the palette of your life. Approach life between its outer edges and you'll discover the joy of nuance."

His mother was probably right. He was nothing if not rational and her words made sense. Still, this way of being, of accepting things he couldn't see, of regarding life as an abstract rather than a still life wouldn't be easy.

"Knock, knock," Chelsea said, leaning into the doorway. "Ronit said to tell you that dinner is almost ready. It smells delicious, by the way. I've had spectacular food here in Israel but this is my first home-cooked meal."

"Well, it's Ina Garten's roast chicken so don't get too excited," his mother said with a smile.

"Wow," Chelsea said, approaching the far wall with its floor-to-ceiling book shelves. "You have so many books."

"We're bookworms here. They don't call us People of the Book for nothing." She winked at Noam.

"Ima...." He groaned like an embarrassed teenager. But Chelsea laughed.

Downstairs, Ronit's kids raced around the dining room table, the boys clinging to their head coverings, each angling for the seat next to their grandfather. Once everyone sat down, Noam's mother began to pass the food.

"Ima, wait," Ronit said.

"Ah, right," said their mother. "Hamotzi." Ronit and her children recited the prayer while Noam, his mother, father and Chelsea remained quiet.

"We're not used to all this religious stuff," Noam's mom said to Chelsea in a mock whisper.

That brought forth an engaging conversation about growing up as a Jew in Texas and Chelsea's upbringing as a Christian in Colorado. Ronit, normally serious and provincial, surprised Noam with her thoughtful questions to Chelsea. It turned out that Ronit read the Tanakh in the mornings just like Chelsea read her scripture cards. Their personal tenets were the same: to love the Lord – Jesus, Hashem – with all their strength, heart and soul. Living faithfully by religious traditions gave both Ronit and Chelsea a comfort they found nowhere else. And they each believed in the depths of their beings that the Messiah would someday return to Israel.

Observing the woman he loved engage easily with his family, Noam thought about the surprising turn his life was taking. He'd been thinking of it as a giant, uncertain leap towards faith. But then he realized it was probably more like a series of tiny shuffles. First, meeting his family. Next, merging their worlds. He wouldn't turn his life over to God, but perhaps someday he could be a co-creator of his life alongside God. His might not be a linear journey, but he had a new willingness to see how it would unfold. Chelsea had given him that.

"We've all seen how faith can tear people apart," his mother was saying.

Noam had lost track of the conversation and hoped that things weren't about to go south. "Jews and Muslims. Evangelicals and liberal atheists. It's tricky. The common thread, which is often forgotten, is that we're all human. And faith is intensely personal."

"That's right," his dad said. "By some standards, even here in Israel, I'm not even Jewish given that my family converted. But I'm a Jew, even though I only go to shul when one of Ronit's children celebrates a bar mitzvah."

"Mine is in four years," Uri chimed in.

"When those differences trouble me, I remind myself of the principle of n'chemta," Ronit added.

"N – what?" Chelsea said.

"N'chemta," she repeated. "It usually refers to Torah stories, many of which can be...daunting or even harsh. N'chemta dictates that Jewish teachings – and life itself – conclude on a hopeful or comforting note."

Underneath the table, Noam took hold of Chelsea's hand. He felt her small bones, her body heat. She squeezed his thigh in a reply of sorts. Noam regarded his family around the table and leaned into the woman he loved. He explained, "N'chemta means that, on principle, stories of the Jews have a happy ending."

"Twelve thousand miles of it, to the other side of the world. And whether they came home again or not, they would belong neither here, nor there, for they would have lived on two continents and sampled two different ways of life."

– Colleen McCullough, The Thorn Birds

Chapter Twenty-Nine

This time, Chelsea knew what to do.

She and Noam had just stowed their carry-ons in the overhead compartment and gathered airplane-issued blankets and pillows for the four-hour flight to Frankfurt where they'd spend a few hours before boarding another flight to Atlanta. They were buckled in and holding hands, an apprehensive excitement shooting between them like a current. Suddenly, from the middle seat, Chelsea looked up and saw the stricken face of an Hasidic man standing in the aisle next to them, glancing down at his ticket and then worriedly back up at the seat numbers above them.

"We can switch!" she nearly shouted. She quickly unbuckled, stood and then swung her hand between herself and Noam. "See? I can move!"

Noam smiled with pride and then stood himself. "Nachleef," he said to the man in Hebrew. *We'll switch seats.* The Hasidic man smiled gratefully at Noam and gave Chelsea a friendlier than expected nod before sliding into the window seat. Noam took the middle and Chelsea settled into the aisle seat.

"You've come a long way since that day on the bus," Noam said, tapping his forehead to hers.

"That feels like a lifetime ago."

"It does," he agreed. "And yet we have a lifetime ahead of us."

Chelsea's whole being buzzed at this thought. To spend her life with Noam, it was...a dream. And yet something that two months ago would have been absolutely unthinkable.

The aircraft backed out of the gate and lumbered towards the runway, its engines whirring to life.

Chelsea looked up at Noam, who was leaning forward to catch a glimpse out the window. "You may be giving up your country," she said, her voice softly cracking, "for me."

He turned to face her. "Israel is a part of my soul whether I'm here or not. Atlanta is our experiment."

"Always a scientist."

"Plus," he added, "you may be giving up your family...for me." The worry and love in his eyes mimicked what she felt. Her mind flitted back to the dinner they'd shared with his family, who'd been so warm and welcoming. There was simply no possibility that her own parents would respond to Noam that way. Not after she'd left Austin. Not after learning he was a Jew. It was indeed possible that she'd lost her family. They were both taking enormous risks, veering their lives in a direction neither could have contemplated before that day they met on a northbound bus in Tel Aviv.

"Yes," she said, both sad and resolute, as the wheels of the plane left the ground. "But I'm gaining a family in you."

》》》》》》》》》》》》》》》》》

WITH THE SCREECH OF THE WINGS SHIFTING, NOAM STIRRED and rubbed his eyes with curled fingers.

"You look like a little boy waking up from an after-lunch nap," Chelsea said, running a hand through his hair. "You slept."

"Yes," he said, blinking at her. "I sleep because you're next to me."

Her eyes shined.

"What have you been doing?" He nodded towards her computer and the yellow legal pad on her tray table. "I thought you'd spend the whole flight reading."

"I finished *The Thorn Birds* last night."

"Your review?"

"Sexy, engrossing. A fascinating examination about a priest who believes he cannot love both a mortal and an immortal."

He nodded.

"So while I'm awaiting the next surprise from my grandmother. I wanted to do a little research. About Atlanta."

"Research? So you're the scientist now?" He winked and she rolled her eyes. "Okay, what have you learned?"

"Well, in addition to the reform synagogues I told you about, Atlanta has a Unitarian church and a Friends Meeting."

He frowned. "For me?"

"No, no," she assured him. "The synagogues are – *may* be – for you, if you choose to explore. The Unitarian church, the Quaker meetinghouse, those are for me to explore. The other night, I re-read part of the Book of Jude, which urges mercy for those who doubt. Witnessing your doubt has forced me to re-examine my beliefs. And I welcome it. My faith feels stronger already."

He took her hand and glanced over the shoulder of the sleeping Hasidic man to his left and out the window to the Frankfurt runway hurtling towards them.

After claiming their bags and clearing customs, they ate in a small restaurant in the terminal.

"I miss Israeli food already," Chelsea said, pushing her plate away after taking a single bite of sloppy, cold goulash. She dug into her backpack for a cinnamon hard candy.

"Sounds like the Atlanta restaurant scene should be your next research topic."

They wandered through the terminal, passing gadget stores, walk-in massage centers and a yoga room. Wordlessly, they stopped before a large door with a black sign bearing white symbols: a cross, the Star of David, a Sanskrit symbol, and a pagoda, among others. They looked at each other and walked inside. There, another sign, translated into several languages, explained that they'd stumbled upon a multi-denominational prayer room, the first in a European airport.

"In Germany, of all places," Chelsea said. "What a contrast from what I saw at Yad Vashem."

The small room, lit mostly by electric candles, featured a plain wooden altar and five rows of pews. It wasn't beautiful but it had a soothing quality, particularly in contrast to the whoosh of humanity in the terminal just outside.

"Let's sit," he said.

Chelsea pulled her navy notebook from her backpack and began reading quietly. Noam took some deep breaths, enjoying just being with her. That he was excited by the unknown of what lay ahead astonished him. They were merging their worlds – their remarkably disparate worlds – and he was willing to simply let it unfold. He was a little anxious, but mostly he was energized. It was a measure of how Chelsea had changed him. And her own willingness to expand her faith beyond Pulpit Springs, the only church she'd ever known, showed that, perhaps, he'd changed her too. Religious beliefs, they'd tacitly agreed, should enhance life, not serve as a barrier to happiness. Their faiths – hers, strong, his, emerging, at best – were wildly different but their connection to each other was far greater than those differences. Neither had to sacrifice, hide or minimize beliefs to be fulfilled together.

After a few minutes, Chelsea closed her eyes and sat quietly. A few minutes after that, she gathered her notebook and pen and returned them to her backpack.

"What did you pray for?" he asked.

"Nothing in particular. I was just talking to God. Doing so reminds me that He's in charge, not me. It helps me stay open to whatever life brings."

"I don't know who's in charge. God – Hashem, Jesus – the Universe or nothing. But however we ended up here...it makes me happy."

"Me too." She kissed his cheek, then turned to face him, her almond eyes shining. "Remember when I told you that Austin qualified his marriage proposal with the words 'next to my faith'?"

"I do."

"What I feel for you...it's not second to anything. I love you like I love God. I love you like I love Hashem."

QUESTIONS
FOR DISCUSSION

1. Could you be romantically linked to someone who observed a different religion or who had no faith at all? Why or why not?

2. Would Chelsea and Noam have fallen in love if their previous relationships (with Austin and Adi) ended amicably rather than by death or cruelty?

3. If you're familiar with the books Chelsea reads or references (*Anna Karenina, Eat Pray Love, Marjorie Morningstar* and *The Thorn Birds*), how well do the themes of those books correlate with what's going on in her life?

4. Do you think Austin and Chelsea's father are true Christians based on what they did after the campaign?

5. What is the difference between Noam and the Hasidics encountered throughout the story – are they all equally Jewish?

6. What's next for Chelsea and Noam? Do you expect they'll stay in Atlanta? Return to Israel? Will their relationship survive their differences in faith and background?

ACKNOWLEGEMENTS

THANK YOU TO THE EARLY READERS OF BESHERT: Tali Levy, Kelli Herzog Anderson, Kerryn Schwarz, Jill Chanen, and Nancy Plasschaert. I'm tremendously grateful for your keen eye, your honesty and your encouragement. Speaking of encouragement, thank you to Amy Mason Doan for serving as both an inspiration and a cheerleader. Extra special thanks go to Maryn Forney, who generously shared her personal journey of faith – I learned so much from you.

The Israelis: Ordinary People in an Extraordinary Land by Donna Rosenthal was a great source of information about Israel and its people.

Thank you to my husband and children – even though I'm a writer, there are truly no words to express how much you mean to me.

ABOUT THE AUTHOR

A "RECOVERING" LAWYER AND LONGTIME LEGAL affairs journalist, Erin Gordon lives in San Francisco. Learn more at ErinGordonAuthor.com.

If you enjoyed this story, the author would be thrilled if you shared your enthusiasm with fellow readers.